BAKER & TAYLOR

ALSO BY DANIEL WOODRELL

Give Us a Kiss
The Ones You Do
Muscle for the Wing
Woe to Live On
Under the Bright Lights

TOMATO
RED

TOMATO
RED

A NOVEL

Daniel Woodrell

A Marian Wood Book

Henry Holt and Company • New York

Henry Holt and Company, Inc.
Publishers since 1866
115 West 18th Street
New York, New York 10011

Henry Holt® is a registered trademark of
Henry Holt and Company, Inc.

Published in Canada by Fitzhenry & Whiteside Ltd.,
195 Allstate Parkway, Markham, Ontario L3R 4T8.

Library of Congress Cataloging-in-Publication Data
Woodrell, Daniel.
Tomato red: a novel / by Daniel Woodrell.—1st ed.
          p.   cm.
"A Marian Wood book."
ISBN 0-8050-5577-0 (alk. paper)
I. Title.
PS3573.06263T66   1998   98-22921
813'.54—dc21   CIP

Henry Holt books are available for special promotions and
premiums. For details contact: Director, Special Markets.

First Edition 1998

Designed by Lucy Albanese

Printed in the United States of America
All first editions are printed on acid-free paper. ∞

1   3   5   7   9   10   8   6   4   2

Anybody possessing analytical knowledge recognizes the fact that the world is full of actions performed by people exclusively to their detriment and without perceptible advantage, although their eyes were open.

—THEODOR REIK

It's not all peaches and cream.
But I haven't learned that yet.

—OIL CAN BOYD

TOMATO
RED

I

Theme Park of Fancy

You're no angel, you know how this stuff comes to happen: Friday is payday and it's been a gray day sogged by a slow ugly rain and you seek company in your gloom, and since you're fresh to West Table, Mo., and a new hand at the dog-food factory, your choices for company are narrow but you find some finally in a trailer court on East Main, and the coed circle of bums gathered there spot you a beer, then a jug of tequila starts to rotate and the rain keeps comin' down with a miserable bluesy beat and there's two girls millin' about that probably can be had but they seem to like certain things and crank is one of those certain things, and a fistful of party straws tumble from a woven handbag somebody brung, the crank gets cut into lines, and the next time you notice the time it's three or four Sunday mornin' and you ain't slept since Thursday night and one of the girl voices, the one you want most and ain't had yet though her teeth are the size of shoe-peg corn and look like maybe they'd taste sort of sour, suggests something to do, 'cause with crank you want something, *anything,* to do, and this cajoling voice suggests we all rob this certain house on this certain street in that rich area where folks can afford to wallow in their vices and likely have a bunch of recreational dope stashed around the mansion and goin' to waste since an article in *The Scroll* said the rich people whisked off to France or some such on a noteworthy vacation.

That's how it happens.

Can't none of this be new to you.

The gal with her mouth full of shoe-peg corn and the bright idea in the first place drives over and lets me off at the curb, and there's another burglar passed out in the backseat who won't be of any help. She doses a kiss out to me, a dry peck on the lips, and claims she'll keep her eyes peeled and I should give the high sign once I've burgled my way inside.

The rain has made the ground skittish, it just quakes and slides away from my footsteps, and this fantastic mist has risen up and thickened so that eyesight is temporarily marked way down in value.

I stumbled into a couple of different hedgerows, one about head high and one around the waist, before I fell onto the walkway. The walkway was, I suppose, made of laid brick, but the bricks were that type that's bigger than house bricks, more the shape of bread loaves, which I think classes them as cobblestones or something. So I wobbled along this big brick walkway, on up the slope and past a lamppost in the yard that made a hepatitis-yellow glow, straight to the backside of the mansion.

Rick folk apparently love their spectacular views, pay dear for them, I'm sure, so there was all this glass. The door was glass and the entire rear wall practically was glass. By sunlight I'd reckon you could see the total spread of the town and long, long pony rides' worth of country-side from any corner in there. All that window gave me brief goofy thoughts of diamond-point glasscutters and suction cups and the whole rigamarole of jewel-thief piss elegance but, actually, with my head out to lunch as it was I just grabbed a few logs from the firewood stack on the patio there and flung them at that glass door.

I suppose I had a sad need to fit in socially with those trailer-park bums, since I imagined they were the only crowd that would have me, because when that first chunk of wood merely bounced from the glass door and skidded across the patio I became bulldog-determined to get the job done for my new friends, and damn the effort or obvious risk.

The logs hit with a bang. Two, three, four times I chucked firewood at that glass and never heard anything close to the sound of a shatter. I sidled up in the mist and skimmed my fingers over the door and felt, I think, the start of some tiny hairline fractures, but there were no big, hopeful splits.

The glass of that door surely had some special qualities that must've been expensive to come by, but worth it, I'd have to say, judging from the wimpy way those logs merely bounced and failed to bust me in there. But I kept pitchin', and bangs kept bangin' out across that neighborhood of mist, until my pitches became tired and wild and I whipped a firewood chunk three or four yards off-line and into a small square window to the flank of the door, and that glass thankfully was of a typical lower order and flew all to pieces.

The glass shatter seemed like a sincere burst of applause, a sincere burst of applause that would come across as alarming and requiring a look-see to any ears open out there in the mist. I went motionless, tried to be a shadow. Pretty quick I heard a derisive shout from shoe-peg mouth, something that might've hurt my feelings to hear clear, then tires squealed and carried my social circle away, leaving me to do the mansion solo.

I stayed a still shadow for a bit, but my mind, such as it was at the moment, was made up and determined: I needed friends, and friendship is this slow awkward process you've got to angle through, and I could yet maybe find what we looked for, return to the trailer park on foot as both a hero and the sudden life of the party.

When no alarm was raised, I came out of my shadow imitation and went to the broken window. The mist felt like a tongue I kept walking into, and my skin and clothes seemed slobbered on. The world aped a harmless watchdog, puttin' big licks all over my face.

The window set too high to spring through, and the glass was not perfectly broken out. There were jaggedy places with long points. I got up on tiptoes and reached my arm through, extra careful, but couldn't reach a latch or doorknob or anything worthwhile.

The batch of flung logs had scattered about and lay underfoot, and the third or fourth time I stumbled on one this thought jumped me. The thought called for a ladder of firewood chunks, and I went to work building this theory that had jumped me from below. That mist made any effort seem sweaty and sweat made me feel employed and that made me start expectin' a foreman to come along and, because of the part in my hair or the attitude of my slouch, fire my ass on a whim, as per usual. But the ladder got built and came to reach the height it needed to.

I think I thought this ladder invention meant I was thinkin' straight.

Atop the ladder I wrapped my T-shirt around my fist and punched the jagged parts loose until there was a clean frame that could be wriggled through without gettin' carved along the flanks.

I slithered inside, uncut, and tumbled among the riches.

My distance perception had gone tilt in my head and that floor reared up and swatted me awful quick. The floor felt like a clean street, a street of that marble stuff, I reckon, maybe Mexican tile, only it was in the kitchen area and mighty stern to land on, especially with that tilt factor in my head, as I barely raised my arms to brace before skidding across it. I'd judged I had further to fall, but huh-uh, and the pain jangle spanned from my elbows and knees to my shoulders and toes. I squealed and rolled and chop-blocked a highback chair in the dark there and sent it tumbling.

You might think I should've quit on the burglary right then, but I just love people, I guess, and didn't.

I became a shadow again, splayed on that imported floor, listening to the mansion. It was supposed to be empty, but newspapers get so many things wrong. Best not to trust them overmuch. The mansion had a slight glow going on inside there, and I got it that they had left a couple of lamps burning in a distant room. The lamps were likely set on a timer and meant to warn away such as I so such as this wouldn't happen.

These burglar lights helped my eyes to focus.

Standing again, finally, I slid my shirt on and rubbed my sore spots, then let my feet aim me toward the glowing room. The crank comedown was settin' in, I think, from the way my feet got heavy and weaved and stomped. This mansion smelled of big achievements and handbags from Rome and unknown treats, which were better scents than I was used to. The walls even seemed special, kind of, as my fingertips skipped along them feeling how fine and costly they felt. My mind, I'd say, stumbled along two or three steps behind my body. More like a waiter than a chef.

When I wobbled inside that lit-up room the wind jumped from my chest. I gasped, groaned, mewed. My legs folded beneath me and I fell face first to a soft carpet that smelled sweeter than my ex-wife's hair and brought to mind sheep in a flowery meadow high in the Alps or Japan or Vermont or some similar postcard spot from out there in the world where the dear goods I'll never own are made.

The sight and smell of all this shook me.

I know I trembled and breathed shallow.

The mansion was the way I'd always feared a mansion would be, only more so. In my fear I'd never managed to conjure the spectacular astounding details. A quick inventory of only this one room made me hate myself. Made me hate myself and all my type that came before me. This mansion was sixteen levels higher than any place I'd ever been among.

As I stared about—gawked, probably—I likely blushed pink to go along with those trembles.

I'd say what such things as I saw in that room were, if I knew the proper names of such things, though I'd bet heavy I've never heard those names spoken. I'm sure such things *have* personal names—those special moody lampshades made of beadwork, and a chair and footstool put together with, like, weaved leather hung on frames of curled iron or polished rare bones, maybe, and end tables that had designs stabbed into them and stuffed with gold leaf or something precious, a small and swank desk over by the far wall, and a bookshelf so old our Revolution must've happened off to the sides of it, carved up with fine points and nicely shined, with a display of tiny statues and dolls arranged just so all across it.

Pretty soon I crawled away from the light, back to the dark parts of the mansion. That sinking feeling set in. Truly, I felt scared, embarrassed for the poorly decorated life I was born to.

This mansion is not but about a rifle shot distant from the trailer park, but it seemed like I'd undergone interplanetary travel. I'd never collided with this world before.

I collected myself in the kitchen. Shuffled my parts back together. My breaths deepened to normal. That splendor had stunned me and then sickened me with a mess of recognitions.

You see the insides of a classier world like that and it sets your own to spinning off-balance, and a tireless gnawing discontent gets to snacking on your guts and spirit. This caliber of a place makes you want to discriminate against yourself, basically, as it reveals you as such a loser. A tiny mote of *nothin' much* just here to muss up the planet these worthies lived so grandly on and wished they could keep clean of you and yours.

I ain't shit! I ain't shit! shouts your brain, and this place proves the point.

Oh, hell yes, this mansion was a regular theme park of fancy fuckin' stuff I never had, never will, hadn't ever truly even seen in person.

Naturally there's some urge to just start smashing amuck in the mansion, whacking all those glamorous baubles and doodads as if these objects had personally tossed you a key ring and told you to fetch their car. That urge is there, to see things shatter, dent, sag with ruin. That urge is always there, usually in shadow though never far away.

But I don't need to want that anymore, or at least lately, so instead I decided to eat.

That mist had gotten bunchy and milled up against the kitchen windows like a rubbernecking crowd peeking in on a private moment. A few wisps shoved in through the busted window and gave me the sense of long fingers slowly pointing.

There was a button on the wall beside the stove, and I punched it and got light. The light pushed the crowd back, slapped away those pointing fingers. This kitchen came near to the size of a decent trailer home. There were, close as I could figure, two stoves or three, or just one giant with a dozen burners. Cabinets ran to the ceiling, made of some blond wood from Oriental lands, I'd guess, and the ceiling was yea tall, so there was a cute li'l stepladder on a runner that slid from cabinet to cabinet so you could see into the upper shelves. A pretty dapper rendition of woodwork, in my opinion. The fridge resembled a bank vault, a big dull metal thing with heavy doors.

The funny thing about these swell folks is they don't leave much food to scrounge. I did a run-through of the fridge and found that all the familiar items were frozen. It disappointed me that there were no exotic leftovers. In the freezer part I turned up a booze bottle that belonged on the pricey shelf at the Liquor Barn. The label on the bottle resembled an eye-test chart, Russian or one of those names, but after a few chugs I could testify it was vodka, for certain, and a quality version of it too.

I began to thrash through the cabinets hunting for peanut butter because I'd seen mayonnaise in the fridge, and peanut butter and mayonnaise meant I could sleep. I could let the crank go bye-bye and sleep. I can't sleep without food nearby. I can't sleep anywhere until I know I'll get to eat again if I need to. I don't have to eat, yet I can't rest without bein' positive sure there's food at hand, but these folks apparently didn't stoop to peanut butter 'cause there wasn't any. Peanut butter is the prescribed hunger medicine for poor folks, and there's always a scraping or so left in the bottom of the jar, somewhere way back in the cupboard. I've been to bed hungry plenty and my tummy whimpered and whimpered and those whimpers are forever on tape in my head.

The vodka at least gave my gut growls instead of whimpers.

Some cheese turned up in the fridge. It's a nice round hunk, but it's not yellow. It's some nearly white kind that smells too gourmet for me, but the hunk was silky smooth and plump as a newborn's rump and I had the sensation of sinkin' my teeth into a pampered baby's butt for a taste.

The flavor was odd but okay, and I knew then I could rest.

The vodka and me and the baby butt of cheese wandered down a dim hall. When crank dies out, a big sudden tired hits, and I could feel it windin' up to smite me. You sleep where you land. I got to a room that echoed as I walked and sounded big, until I bumped my shin on a chair, then fell into it, and threw my head back and raised my feet to the stool out front.

My collapse had been into a calfskin wingback chair, and I just folded into it, tucked myself away secretly there like a French tickler in a gentleman's leather wallet.

The dreams that made the scene inside my skull weren't dreamy dreams, but rather more like long news clips from kangaroo court sessions convened on me in a gaudy plush holding cell, and the entire jury was made up of loved ones I'd sorely disappointed since they were buried and whiskery perverts who took a shine to me just the way I was.

I slept for over a full day, as you know, but I won't say I rested.

2

Tuxedo Swallowed

I fell deep down in there, until this bright light raised me from sleep. Coming out of a pit such as that, you think the bright light could be God or a cop on patrol; then your brain wakes up to where you think you are and there's a train light bearing down on you; then my eyes got right and it was just a candle held in front of my face by a girl in a black gown with jewelry twinkling here and there and a young fella in a tuxedo that swallowed him, smoking a heavy white pipe with a face design sculpted around the bowl.

"Are you dangerous?" the girl asked. "You look dangerous."

I went to rub my face, slap myself wide awake, but my arms didn't work, and I looked down and saw straps of silver tape wedding me to that chair. There wasn't much wiggle room.

"I went without sleep too long, that's all."

This girl stood about five foot flat in spike heels and didn't weigh much more than an ancient one-armed butler could carry. In that candlelight she came across as tiny, but hard and fluttery too.

"We're interested in dangerous types."

"I probably need to shave and whatnot. Hit the showers."

The fella had my wallet in his hands and was helping himself to my personal papers. That pipe clenched in his teeth went *boing-boing* like a diving board. He didn't draw much smoke, I noted. The face on that pipe was lean and goateed and maybe satanic, a face you hope to not see in a detox situation. I thought I recalled that pipe from the bookshelf in the lighted room.

"You look awfully like the man," she said, "we were starting to think about looking for."

"He would make that appearance with less beard," the fella said. "Or, mayhaps, a good deal *more* beard."

She reached over and flicked a lamp on. I appeared to be in a den. The ceiling was way up there for a house, eighteen or twenty feet at least. Dead things had left their heads on the walls. Across the room I saw a pale stone fireplace you could walk into without slouching hardly.

"Are you frightened?" she asked.

"I haven't peed my pants yet," I said. "But then, it's been a while between beers."

"He just might do," the fella said. "He's got that 'born to lose and lose violently' air about him. That's good."

The two of them made a sight. I hate to fall back on *weird* to describe them, but *goofy* is too weak, and *strange* sounds too sensible.

"What's your story?" she said.

First off, her hair was red, a shade of red that would be natural on something growing in a garden but not on a person's head. Her hair was cut in this real, real short yet ruffled manner that's likely up to the minute, style-wise, off in other places, and costs plenty, I'm sure. The hair is short enough for an old-time marine but still somehow styled to give off loads of womanly oomph. That tomato-red hair was accompanied by fancy-pants ghoul makeup. She sported lipstick that I'd call graveyard black, and her fingernails could've been dead-baby blue. All this made her look hep to it all, jack, and a good bit foreign. Her eyes were of that bossy gray hue, born to issue orders and have them followed to the letter.

I wasn't instantly up for meeting new people, but no use in being rude. Friends come from anywhere.

"I don't have much of a story, really."

"Surely you do. Tell us."

I thought about trying a few themes out on them, such as: I'd been rich once too, had my own waffle house, say, but I wouldn't pay off the Dixie Mafia so they burned me out; I'd been the number-seven middleweight contender until I got two detached retinas in a yacht fiasco you probably saw on the news; I was a kick-around mutt from Blue Knee, Arkansas, with a file number, on my own slow ramble throughout sincere poverty and various spellbinding mishaps.

The fella spared me my breath. He read from my driver's license. The tuxedo sleeves ran down beyond his fingertips and had to be shoved back every breath or two. He kept that pipe in his teeth and kept it hopping as he spoke.

"Barlach," he said, and he pronounced it with "lack" at the tail, which is how I say it, but lots don't at first. "Sammy. He's twenty-four, from the great state of Arkansas—which means he's over seventeen miles outside his homeland—claims to be six feet two inches tall and to weigh one-seventy. Blond and brown."

"That's helpful," she said. "But it doesn't tell us if he's dangerous."

"Looky here," I said. "I'm not truly that dangerous, I'm just sort of nutsy actin', that's all."

She and him both began to slowly move around me, studying me close. They went *hmm*, and *mm-hmm*, and *uh-huh*. It hit me that I stunk and stunk fairly high, and likely didn't seem an affable figure at all. They each smelled nice and seemed cordial.

"He could easily be remade to *look* dangerous," the fella said. "It wouldn't take much. Wrap him in a few he-man fashion clichés, give him a new hairdo."

"Yes," she said. She sat on the arm of my chair then, and I saw she held a kitchen knife loosely in her left hand. The blade displayed a row of mean-spirited teeth. "Awfully, awfully dangerous. Oh, goodness gracious, yes, he could be made to pass for a *mighty* bad man."

"Do we trust him enough to cut him loose?" the fella asked.

"A close call," she said. "He's still pretty sleepy but he *is* a housebreaker, a thief."

"I wouldn't steal *valuables*," I said. "I'm not *that* way. I only take nonsense stuff. You know: household drugs, neckties that blink or wave or have hula girls on them, that sort of silly shit. Snapshots of your wife gettin' undressed, maybe any ol' rockabilly music or gut-bucket blues you accidentally still got layin' around." The vodka bottle sat on a table behind the pair of them, and I took note it was empty. "And, okay, I'll drink your liquor too. But, all in all, I'm not actually an outright *thief* type."

The fella had wandered over to where I could totally see him, face on, in decent light, and how he looked— well, it ain't easy for me to say out loud.

He's the kind of fella that if he was to make it to the top based only on his looks you'd still have to say he deserved it. Hoodoo sculptors and horny witches knitted that boy, put his bone and sinew in the most fabulous order. Dark-haired, green-eyed, with face bones delicate and dramatic both. If your ex had his lips you'd still be married. His size was somewhat smallish, but he was otherwise for certain the most beautiful boy I ever had seen. I'm afraid "beautiful" is the only word I can make work here, and I'm not bent or nothin', but beautiful is the truth.

"God damn," I said, looking at him.

That comment probably sounded like a gasp.

The girl grinned at me, looked at him, beamed, and giggled.

"Isn't he something?" she said. "Grown women at the grocery store toss him their panties with their home phone numbers marked on in lipstick."

"Quit it," he said. "Don't start in on me."

"Tsk, tsk." That knife was yet notably in her tiny hand, and not still. "Sammy," she went, "I'm Jamalee, and this squire here is my baby brother, Jason."

I strained at my straps some, then nodded.

"I'd shake, but . . ."

She leaned her face to mine, put her eyes six inches from mine, and stared. She was drilling something potent into me. She drilled it in deep.

"I hope this is for the best." She put the blade to the strap across my chest and began to saw. Her eyes held steady and drilled past my crust to where I get gooey. "It seems I'm always doin' the *noble* thing," she said softly, "then regrettin' it."

3

Double Everything

Chances such as this come few and apart.

Jamalee and Jason introduced me to a bathroom upstairs that had a vast and nifty tub, with sort of a bench, even, underwater. You could stretch out, float, flop around, or sit on that slick bench in the hot bubble bath and have a deep think. I sank in among the steam and bubbles and lathered and scrubbed and dunked. When I climbed out there was this silk, or something of the silk type, robe for me to wear. The robe was the blue of a peacock fan. I found a blade, shaved clean at the sink. Six or eight flavors of cologne were on a stand there, and I splashed on one I never heard of, Vetiver, and the smell was fancy and wonderful.

This whole sequence was like a crazy dream you seem to understand.

I wore only that robe and my new smell back downstairs. The stairs went this way, then that way, then the other way again, and it amounted to a short dizzy hike. The kids didn't have things too bright on the first floor. They seemed to enjoy candles but not lightbulb light. Three candles sat on a table and burned and cast a wavy sort of spiritual light that belonged at a séance or in a van when you're undergoing sex.

I came into the dim light, and shadows had got up and were bucking and winging real festive across the walls. The pair of my new buddies sat at a long thick table with probably crystal wine goblets set out. The wine looked black. I noted three goblets.

She said the first words.

"We'd like to hire you."

"Oh, now, I've *got* a job." There was a shovel with my name on it in the burn room at the dog-food factory, but my name was only on a piece of gray tape that had already come a little loose at the edges. I'd made several sizable promises to get that shovel job. My work history was awful spotty, see, even with all the shit I invented to shove into the blank periods. "A pretty good one, too."

"That's nice," she said. "It's not what I want to hear, but it's nice for you. This job, though. Do you work on Mondays?"

"Well, sure. Through Fridays."

"Oops," went Jason.

"Did you call in this morning, say you were sick?"

I reacted with a stare at her.

"Today's Sun—"

"Huh-uh, Sammy," she said. Her tomato head swayed about. "Sorry about this, but it is now approaching a fashionably late dinner hour on Monday evening. You overslept by half a day, I'm afraid."

I took a seat at the table. I put my fingers to my ears and yanked and yanked until my eyes pooled and my brain snapped to attention. The foreman had barely hired me in the first place.

"I'm starvin'," I said.

I stood away from the table, shuffled barefoot to the kitchen. Their footsteps followed close behind me. I got back there where all the glass and the great view were, and there was nothin' but dark caused by heavy clouds and whipping rain all across the landscape. Big plump trees were waddling in place. I stood silent, quite a long minute or two, staring out, listening to the mud grow.

"Let's microwave a dinner for Sammy," Jason said lightly. "Him needs a hot meal."

I couldn't bother to watch.

That bank vault broke open with a suck noise, and he shoved around in the frozen food section, then shut the door.

"How does clam linguini sound?"

I spun around then, and went on and gave in, gave in all the way to who I was.

"Now I always have loved that dish," I said, hoping I actually would, "whenever it's been served."

We got along real quick.

The two of them held candles and showed me about the mansion, escorting me from room to room. I still only wore that peacock-blue robe and a high-toned smell, yet this scene came across like a job interview, more or less. They had recruited me to be "security." I was to adjust my criminal insights around to where I could defend the mansion, and the family of the mansion, from anything else of my stripe that might come along. They'd flick on a light at each room for a short burst, then flick it off and say "piano room" or "the squire's room," "tea parlor," "maid's suite."

This place, even seen in short bright moments, was revealed to have double of everything worth having, just about.

Looking at this place I could understand how tremendous a responsibility it amounted to, and I was thinking that probably I could work for folks with their pluses.

Now these two had presented themselves as savvy youths and seemed that and more, even, because they'd been exposed to most of the world and studied on it from a lofty, sharp angle. I knew the Delta up and down, and the Ozarks a good bit, Memphis of course, and had took a big taste of Houston once; but everywhere I knew, I knew only the lower-priced, fewer-questions-asked parts of. They, though, ran down a few casual memories to me about Greece (the bright white islands and topless crowds), Tokyo (you needn't wash your own self in the hot tubs over there, no sir), London (best bring an umbrella), and their second home, Paris (where the chefs all knew their birthdays and sprang parties on them with these delicate celebration foods I'd never come across and might not have the balls to eat).

We came to a large window that had large panes at the end of the staircase, and there was a jumbo vase with some sort of plumes towering out, and over to the side of it was a black door that Jamalee pushed open and found a switch and lit the room. She looked at the olden bed with a posh canopy and at the walls coated with mirrors and artwork, and dear wooden furniture.

"This," she said, "will be your room, Sammy."

I gave that room a once-over and had a flush dart up to my head, out to my ears.

It was as though I had busted into a dark mansion and somehow woke up inside the dream I *should've* been dreaming my whole life long.

Jason slid from the room and down the hall, and I said to her, "For real? This room is really, really choice. A choice fuckin' room."

Her eyelids had shadow laid on so heavy it seemed she peered at me from two blue knotholes. Her face, Jamalee's face, had already plopped down into my mind like a hook.

"Now," she started, "if in any way it's not—"

That's when Jason jumped into the room, blew out her candle and his own, and said, "The law is out there with flashlights. Time to choo-choo, Sis."

Jamalee's response was she laughed wide open. Her sound vibrated the blackness. She beat my back and laughed toward my ear. She enjoyed this moment, the moment when danger has arrived and I'm revealed as a cranked-out dipshit. It's for the best that I couldn't see her expression.

"That's never goin' to be my room, is it."

4

Don't Fun Me

Panic put wings on our feet. The flashlights of the law beamed behind us and not far. I had my hands in my cowboy boots up to the elbows and my true clothes were pinched in my armpit. Their true clothes were in a tote bag; they'd been prepared for this event. Mud grabbed at us up to the ankles. My feet were bare. Our six feet flew through the fresh mud, and the mud tagged along in flecks and speckles on legs, hands, faces, hair. At this speed that bathrobe flapped wide and exhibited me. Each step down into and up out of the mud emitted a sound like something starved chased one step behind, smacking its lips.

Mist hung in heavy drapes and made every direction a

question mark to me. Jamalee and Jason knew where we were and how to exit and I did not contain that knowledge. Jamalee set the style, leading us in a furtive-monkey sort of scoot, bent low so any silhouettes blended into the blot of the dark ground, then a sudden scurry from this tree to that bush to the hedgerow and escape.

Now, you listen, here's a key point: Despite this moment of panic and flight, and everything else, I never did get it deleted entirely from my assessment of this pair that they were smart, important rich kids. I knew the truth on one hand, but I'd been so *moved* by the lie! That lie had been good to believe, and it lingered and lingered as that type of lie is wont to do.

All I could do was follow.

Along the route these things were said:

"Vassar, my ass. You ever even finish high school?"

"When I left high school you can be *sure* I was finished with it."

"Hey, cowboy, don't you wear underwear?"

"I guess I was robbed while I slept."

"Hold your robe shut, then. Be decent."

"That's too much strain."

"We truly live in Venus Holler."

"Oh, yeah? My mom left home just before I was born."

"We do. Truly. Merridew is our name."

"You could bunk with us. There's a spare bunk in my room. Sis'n me, we really could use 'security.'"

"Huh-uh. I get misguided over and over on my own. With you two I'd be nothin' but."

"But I forget things, Sammy. I could use you to help me keep the nightmare straight."

"Don't fun me. Don't fun me again, or I'll have me a bad spell that'll be *worse* for you-all. I'll whip you and anything that *re*-minds me of you."

"See, Sis? Isn't he great? He's just the greatest!"

"What'd I just tell you?"

"He's *perfect*. He's *i*-deal."

The mud petered out, and we hit the shoulder of a concrete creek. Water ran along deep at a high speed and hissed as it passed. We came to a bridge over this drainage ditch and switched clothes beneath it.

It was bad light under there, but we all stripped down to where our skins dappled the gloom, and moved about, ghostly, of course.

I didn't have my shirt anymore.

They both had complete changes in that tote bag.

My socks had slipped away, so it was raw muddy feet I tugged my boots onto.

Jason tossed me the tuxedo jacket and I wore it over my bare chest.

Not much was said, but when something was, I answered, "The other way from you."

5

All That Human Juice

I still can get lost. West Table, Mo., is such a big town compared to Blue Knee, where I was grown, down in Arkansas. That's about an hour and a tall beer to the Delta side of Little Rock. Sixty Blue Knees'd fit into this town here and still have leftover citizens to loaf around the edges.

Blue Knee only held about a hundred souls and naturally I was required to know every damn one of them. In this town I can shuffle in the crowd and scarcely need to nod. So privacy can be had here in the hills, but it gets crossbred with loneliness, too. These Ozarkers don't overwhelm strangers such as me with ready backslaps and quick invitations.

Some places I could find, such as the trailer court, which I reached about midnight in a small quiet rain. My wheels sat there, parked on the chat and pea-gravel lane beside the trailer I thought I'd begun this recent backslide in. My car was black, a sun-beaten black, an old Ford, the make that explodes into a fireball now and then. The car's not big or strong, more runty and sputtering. It's like driving a pregnant roller skate. The tape deck worked.

The windows were clouded on the inside, and drops beaded and burst and ran down the glass. I held the door open with a boot toe so the overhead light would stay on. Things that should've been there had gone absent and left bare spots in the mess. Several special pieces of clutter had left the scene, and I wanted them back.

I reached under the seat, into the springs, and felt the holster. The empty holster. I'd gotten shed of that popgun, I suddenly recalled. The danger in me having a pistol handy had mounted and mounted and blessed me with insights toward the future—some mean bumpkin in a juke joint shoves me and that spills bourbon and cola on my favorite shirt, the pale blue one with the chopped collar and the history of supplying good luck, pussy-wise, and I become a lunatic for three and a half minutes and decide I've just *got* to kill me a bumpkin to avenge that stained shirt. Such insights came in too clear. I sold the pistol to a pretty temperamental Indian in a casino parking lot at Tunica, Mississippi, more than a month back.

I'm not certain I was glad I'd come to my senses that way when I went toward the trailer door. The tux jacket had gotten soaked and hung on me and weighed me down like some shackle I did to myself 'cause I thought it had style. Lights were on in the trailer, and I might have merely driven away had I not heard the music—Groovey Joe Poovey singing "Careful Baby."

I gave the door a couple of thumps.

The window curtains wiggled and I saw a hand.

Two more thumps and the door opened.

I looked at the man who was wearing a Sun Studio Memphis hat, and said, "First off, fat boy, that's *my* hat."

"Who you think you're talkin' to, punk?"

"A fat boy wearin' my hat, that's who."

Back among my own element I know how to be. You've got to show your teeth and show them plenty.

The music had shifted to Rudy Tutti Grayzell, and I added, "And that's my music."

"That's your shit car out there? I just about sold it to the scrap man this mornin', but he wouldn't come up to a ten-dollar bill on it." He had an audience available behind him, which snorted.

This boy was short and bearded and not a great citizen. I had a slight hazy recollection of the bum. His gut was like a greedy kid's Halloween sack on a Halloween when it didn't rain cold rain to keep down the harvest. He had a front on him, an image thing, a look and demeanor that tried to sell you on the notion that you best walk softly near this bad tubby 'cause he's evil, baby, a special brand of slippery fat evil.

I went up the three steps fast and pushed inside, and he seemed confused.

"I believe I'll collect my tapes—and right now."

There was a fella on the couch, the sort of small, skinny alcoholic redneck who probably had a cannon in his sock and an undertaker for a brother-in-law. A female slumped against him, and she was exactly the type you'd expect to find in this trailer with these fellas.

I pushed the eject button on the music box and found the case for that one tape right away. There were tapes scattered all over, on the floor, on the TV trays, next to the scuzzy sink.

"Buddy," fat boy said, "you're really advertisin' for an ass-whuppin', ain't you?"

He'd gotten close. I'd already found some tunes—

Wanda Jackson, Champion Jack D., Sleepy LaBeef, Magic Slim, Ronnie Hawkins, Carl Perkins, The Killer, and The King—but I dropped them of a sudden and hit him. This is one of the worst traits of us. His mouth busted to pulp and all that human juice dashed over his cheeks and beard, then began to drip down his neck, inside his shirt.

It's the way of our world, which is the one world I know.

The little alcoholic didn't reach for a cannon. He reached for a coffee cup of whiskey and silently saluted me with it.

The female said, "Have a seat, why don't you?"

"Huh-uh. I ain't had all my shots."

There was a trash bag there, and I tossed my tapes into it, and maybe a couple of tapes not strictly mine (I'd been trying to find pleasure in typical dinosaur rock, really trying), and walked to the door. I looked back and fat boy was leaned over the sink, leaking himself into it, swirling down the drain.

I crossed the room again and snatched my hat from his hairy head.

"I don't have hardly nothin', man," I said, "and you're stealin' from *me*! I can't abide that. I can't abide that at all, conscience-wise. It puts really wrong pictures in my head, man." At the door I stopped and

added, "You *could* let yourself learn from this, you
know?"

Then home. I had a room with no cooking privileges
on Hyde Street where it snakes sideways across the hill
above the square. It was a squat old and gabled sort of
place, with separate rooms devised and jerry-rigged every
which way. You'd discover some tiny, tiny nook off the
kitchen and it would turn out to be some geezer's world.
The social atmosphere tended to be like a wake, sort
of, only today's corpse hadn't quite been settled on
yet. Whenever you'd hear a fellow boarder hack and
wheeze and shuffle down the hall to tap a kidney or
puke, you'd hope aloud you wouldn't be the one who
found him at dawn, stiff and purple, jackknifed over the
crapper.

Mrs. Soose collected the rent and set the tone. She was
one of those unhappy, even miserable older gals who've
found the entire planet to be a disappointment and go
around all the time fretting and wondering just why Mr.
Mysterious Ways has kept them alive and on earth for so
terrible a long time. Probably she was only about sixty, but
she'd done hard time every day and I won't even think
about her nights.

My room was up the first rank of stairs and toward

the back. The front-door key worked fine, but the room key stuck. I gave several twists and kicked the bottom of the door a time or seven. It seemed, I guess, that the rain and humidity had gotten to my door and warped it shut.

I was contemplating a jump across the lower roof and a wet crawl to my one window when there she was, in pale pink terry cloth and face cream.

"Hey, Mrs. Soose, my door's stuck."

"The lock's been changed, Mr. Barlach. There's the matter of the two weeks' rent you guaranteed me on Friday last. When you got your first paycheck."

I thought fast of a pack of lies but didn't bother to say them. Mrs. Soose had heard all the lies of all the renters since before I'd been old enough to beat with a fist. My lies would hit her like spit, and she'd just wipe and get mad and stay mad.

"And your foreman—see, I called to see if you'd died in a wreck or somethin'—he told me you ain't got a job no more."

Anyway, blah-blah, I've slept in the Ford before. I took the wet tuxedo off, found a smelly shirt on the backseat. It was the light blue one with the chopped collar and the bourbon and cola stain.

I parked in the lot at Happy Bark Dog Food. The time of year was spring, and April was trying to drown this region, as usual. I opened the glove box and there was half a candy bar and a small bag of smoked almonds. So I could rest.

I pulled the rearview down and looked at myself in the mirror for a spell, trying to spot virtues.

Then I put my head back.

When the sun rose, don't you know, I intended to find out if I could beg.

6

Lain Unrepaired and Become

Venus Holler was the most low-life part of town, so I already knew where it was. I stalled until late afternoon before I let myself drive down there. I felt instantly at home.

What I came to know: Venus Holler as a name was one of those cruel country jokes that sticks. It was a holler of small, square homes that leaned sideways a bit like a bunch of drunks who can't quite hear each other. The holler naturally lay across the tracks from the decent citizens of West Table, but so barely across the tracks that trains made these joints quiver. If a train passed at breakfast time, all the eggs ended up scrambled. There was an awful chunky road through the holler, a road that had been paved out of pity once back in the bygones but had busted up over the years and lain unrepaired and become forever rugged. The houses have their roofs pulled down low over the front stoops, like hats worn at a sulky angle over hungry, stubbled faces. Back in the heydays this was where the whores all had to live, the whores who serviced all the cattlemen and pig farmers who shipped their stock from West Table and went on toots during their visits, as well as the local lovelorn. The name got to be Venus Holler, I'm told, precisely because a goddess is the very last dame you'd ever expect to find there—but if ever you did, for three bucks you could fuck her too.

I followed directions, knocked at the door.

The rain had rolled on and a freewheelin' sun toured the sky. I looked around as I waited. The ridgeline makes this holler mighty hard to gaze up out of. It keeps your vision on what's held in the holler and shunts the eye from all else. This is the kind of address where the wives will know shortcuts to the welfare office and have a bail bondsman's home phone number taped to the fridge.

I heard footsteps and knocked again.

If this house was meat you'd let the dog eat it.

The footsteps arrived and the inside door jumped back. Someone was there, but the screen was between us.

"You're not on time," this woman's voice said. "You'll have to have a seat. Come on in, hon—there's beer in the kitchen."

She disappeared before I could see her, but her smell stayed behind to introduce her to me. The smell, I'd say, came from mimosa. A mimosa species of smell, anyhow.

Inside, the place pulled itself together, stood up straight, showed some effort. Everything was passably clean, and the furniture had slipcovers with cheerful designs in cheerful colors.

I decided not to be standoffish. I went into the kitchen, which was easy to find since there were only two ways to turn from the front room, and she hadn't gone to the kitchen and her smell tracked to the left, to a bedroom, I now know. The fridge contents proved this was a gal's fridge—a box of white wine, the kind with a spigot, yogurt all over the place, vegetable juice, and one li'l palm-sized minute steak. I wondered what Jason might eat, or did he eat the same. The beer was on the bottom shelf, in bottles, and it was your standard prominent St. Louis brand of beer.

And that made it just fine.

She called, "You're not dressed how I expected. I think you spilled somethin' on your shirtfront, there. But you should be at your ease, hon—that's the way things come out for the best."

I guzzled the first beer at the sink, there, just totally defeated that bottle in two fierce chugs. I grabbed another from the fridge, feeling a little bit goosed and hopeful, then drifted to the front room.

A painting on the wall was wide and showed smudged flowers and smudged lily pads on a funny-colored pond. A decent-standing walnut display case was cut to fit into the corner, and it had been crammed with cocktail glasses that said where they were from: Brennan's, Cal-Neva Lodge, The Vapors, Harold's Club, Stan and Biggie's, The Arlington, The Peabody, Old Absinthe House, Tootsie's Orchid Lounge—and so on for maybe twenty mai tais more.

"I need help. I had to change when I saw you. Which shoes do you favor, hon?"

This woman stood there, blond, in jeans and a thin clingy pink blouse. She held a pair of shoes in each hand.

I didn't speak up, so she did.

"I have these, my nice comfortable flats, or *these*, my tall *fuck-me, fuck-me, fuck-me* heels. Which do you favor?"

"Well . . ."

"Oh, why am I askin' you? I *know* what *you* think—but the flats are so much more sensible for when we dance, hon."

The woman tossed the pair I would've chosen off somewhere, put the other on.

She was one of those gals who look like they've patterned theirselves after a child's doll. A Barbie who has gone to seed on roadhouse whiskey and panfried chicken. I'd put her age at plenty old enough, but not yet too old. Thirty-five, or maybe forty, but not much over that. She had a big smell, big hair, big smile.

"It's less awkward," she said, and sidled close up to me, "if you present my gift to me now, and I'll hide it away, and that will be all we'll say about that."

"Might this gift be a cash gift?"

That big smile stepped aside, then she snapped a cigarette between her lips and lit it with a thin golden lighter.

"If you're not Steve Jimmerson's brother-in-law from Cape Girardeau, then A, you owe me for the beer, and B, you better quick say something sweet that doesn't scare me. I'm *easily* frightened."

"A mistake was made," I said. "That's all. Look here, now, I—you know—I went into that store up the road there, Lake's Market, I think they call it, or somethin', and they directed me here. The man at the counter. What I'm lookin' for is this tiny red-haired girl, said her name was Merridew, which is the name I asked after at the store. They said knock here."

About this instant she had things sorted out. Her eyes narrowed and her lips twitched as if a mocking laugh was getting into position to spring forth.

"Now how did she get her hooks into a rugged ol' *long, tall* cowpoke like you?"

"I met her, that's all."

"She's not *be*-guiling. She doesn't bother to be *a*-ppealing, not often, not often that I ever did see."

"She's got a way, though, that comes across—to me, at least."

"Does she now? Think you might could get a li'l of that cotton, do you?"

"Never say never."

"Jamalee is my daughter—did you know?"

"Naw. Naw."

"I'm Bev Merridew—that's why Tim sent you to the wrong house. You say Merridew around here and that's usually *me*. Not far off, though, it's goin' to always be Jason, I imagine."

I did the beer in. I wasn't sure what to do with the bottle.

"He's a right glamorous boy—I can testify to that."

She sucked and blew smoke, gave me an up-and-down look the way a warden might when he was deciding which tier to jail you on.

"No," she said, and shook her head. "No, huh-uh, you're not, I can tell. Not *you*, cowboy."

She beckoned me to a side window, and I stood there and got rocked by her smell and smoke and sharp savory possibilities that were dangled merely by her posture and presence.

"Right there," she said, and pointed to the next house over. "Jam and Jason stay there, close by but out of my hair. They're old enough."

The next house over was like a reflection of this one in a dented mirror that had been settled on by dust.

"Scoot. I've got a caller droppin' by any hot minute now, and *you* can't be here. So *ske*-daddle."

At the doorstep I turned back to the screen, which had been tragic for quite a few flies that were squished there, and added, "My name is Sammy Barlach, and growing up I always kept chickens—so you *know* I'm a good lover."

These were those households of the awful fully shared. I parked in the mud-rut driveway. I knew such places by heart. Everything fine or wonderful got hoarded each to his own, but the miserable shit passed around and around and up and down.

A yellow bus honked on the road and went by, carrying a load of tired young Baptists home from the Bible camp that sat four or five miles down. There were two babes in rusty-lookin' diapers wrestling with a dog in a mud yard across the street. Mom squatted on the porch, cherishing her cigarette, and there was a squad of dead schnapps soldiers scattered to the side of the steps.

I soon changed my mind, stepped out of the Ford, and went over to Jamalee's door. I could see she stood inside the screen door, watching me. The screen had been given a rounded, pooched-out shape by insiders leaning into it, headfirst, pushing a little farther out each time, hoping for some slightly improved view, I guess.

"Well, look what the rain washed by," she said. "Didn't expect to see you."

"Aw, I ain't goin' nowhere in life anyhow, so I might as well get there this way."

"Oh, baby, do *I* feel *that* theory." She came in a step closer to the screen, which put her face to use as an attraction. "What about your job, Sammy?"

She eased on out the door, to the slumped wood floor of the stoop, and held the screen open with her hip. There was no makeup now. Her hair had been wetted and combed down slick.

"I'm gettin' it back," I said. "With a hike in pay, too, and a few special fringe benefits. The man said I'll be startin' the very next day after hell freezes over."

"That sounds promising."

She stepped backwards, into the house, and let the door shut between us. It was passing strange how different she looked in her own true clothes and her own true home, swaddled in her own true history. A big share of her sparkle dulled as that pooched-out screen door slammed her inside.

Then she moved backwards, deeper into the shadow. All I could see was that she was barely there, like something you almost recall: the Pledge of Allegiance, your daddy's real name.

"Come on in, Sammy. Share the stink."

7

Transferred to a Period

Jamalee and Jason were living together like a brother and sister who'd maybe once tended to play a lot more "Doctor" together than is considered sightly. They acted familiar with areas of each other that most siblings probably keep private, but this knowledge seemed to bond them together even better instead of wedging them apart.

The house was nearly a coop; you could've paced it off and counted the paces on fingers and toes. Jamalee had set up housekeeping in the dining nook, closed her zone in with a blanket curtain hanging from a clothes-line she'd hammered to the walls. Jason had an actual room with a double-deck of bunk beds in it. He gave me the top, which is the new inmate's rack in so many circumstances.

I made do.

I always have just wanted to fit in somewhere, and this is the bunch that would have me.

The house belonged to a timber hauler who worked off the books and only showed his face two or three times a month to crash in my bunk. He was yonder and all over knockin' down forests and hauling them to sawmills. His wife had hit the highway and taken the three kids with her. They'd been holding those kids as hostages to the welfare machine and drawing decent ransom checks. His name was Rod, and Rod wanted those checks to keep coming, so he'd installed Jamalee to answer the phone and mimic his woman. A piece of paper had been taped to the wall above the phone, and it had files, sort of, on his kids: birth dates, eye colors, school situations, excuses: so Jamalee could talk straight to any social welfare snoops.

She got a cut, but I don't think a big one. Her main reward was the free inhabiting of this coop.

The Merridew kids shared the coop with Rod's dog. It was a shaggy, lazy dog named Biscuit who had the personality of a defeated old alcoholic uncle, more or less. Biscuit mainly just laid there and thumped his tail pleasantly.

Once in a while he goes to the screen door and stands there scanning the street like he's hopin' to see the mailman bringing his disability check, then moans in disappointment and flops back down.

It was as though I'd never left, I'd always been here.

Jam and me split a cream soda on the porch stoop that first afternoon. Bev came strolling out from next door on the arm of a fella who was hard to remember. There was nothing to him at all except a green suit jacket and a Japanese car.

"I reckon your mom's payin' the utilities with that fella."

"We don't say mom, we say Bev." There was a sharp bite to her sentence. "Bev's a porcupine, Sammy. Know what that is?"

"I've heard this one, but I forgot."

"If Bev had all the dicks that've been stuck *in* her stickin' *out* of her, she'd look like a goddam porc-u-pine."

The man held the car door for Bev. She'd put on a nice print dress and those tall heels. I thought she gave us a glance, a short fox glance over the shoulder.

"Yeah," I said. "That's it. I'd forgot the punch line."

"You want to keep your distance from her."

Jam's comment made no nevermind with me.

I'm not the type who can exclude people socially just because they operate under some bad habits.

She, it turned out, had recently gotten to be nineteen, and he was about a quarter past seventeen. They'd felt as pointless in school as I had. Jason was an apprentice hairdresser at Romella's, on the square. After so many hours and days of experience he could take the test to become licensed. Beyond that, see, Jamalee would manage a shop for him, not here but someplace in the high cotton, where folks spent money just so they didn't have to carry it around anymore, and the rich ladies got snickered at if they didn't have a beautiful boy "escort" that they were seen everywhere with.

Apparently this region was thought to exist either in the Beverly Hills area or south Florida.

Romella's Salon was where the kids heard who of note might be out of town when, and broke into the houses of these customers of note and had practice sessions at acting well-to-do. They needed to learn a way to seem natural surrounded by plush, since plush was where they were aimed. Jamalee immediately set out to rebuild my front, get me facing in the direction she wanted to go.

"I believe I'll call you Samuel."

"No. I'm a Sammy. Always have been."

"But Samuel rings more like an adult."

"It ain't my name."

"But Sammy as a name is a person that can only wash and wax the cars, whilst a *Sam-u-el* might own the dealership."

"My ma named me Sammy. It's what's on my birth certificate."

"Really? Truly? She named you Sammy? Flat-out Sammy?"

"She sure did."

"Taggin' that name on you, that was like casting a curse on you. Oh, baby, your ma made a sorry, shitty prediction on your whole life and hung a name on you that would help the sorry, shitty stuff come true."

"You ain't bringin' me any news."

"We can see that you're not all bad," Jamalee said, "but we hope you're bad enough."

This was the second of our days together, or maybe more than that. It could've been that second day, or a week later, but anyhow she and me were sitting in the waiting area at Romella's, waiting on Jason.

"I'm not sure *bad* is the label I want."

This was my first glimpse of Jason's magic; there were three gals waiting for him to be free. They ignored the girl hairwashers and sat in a quiet, expectant row, waiting for Jason to scrub their heads, which at this stage was the most of what he was allowed to do. You could see their faces as his fingers worked across their scalps, ran through their wet hair, kneaded above their temples, and the expressions the gals displayed belonged over a diamond that wasn't fake or during the first licks of love. Probably no man had touched their heads before who they weren't "serious" with.

"I'm a bad girl myself, Sammy," Jamalee said, "but not that many people get the benefit of it."

"I prefer the word 'rugged.' Or 'difficult.' "

"You're both, baby, if that's what you want."

I kept an eye on Jason and, great balls of fire, that boy would be worth his weight in tips, almost daily. He had a spiffy future beggin' for him to come on in, beautiful, and have all of what I've got.

"Let me tell," Jamalee said, leaning my way, her little hand resting on my forearm, "our plans."

This girl was tiny and relentless. Her head looked like an heirloom tomato after a rough, scrubbing cloudburst. If ever I could possess a '65 Mustang, four-speed ragtop, I'd want it to be the color of her hair.

"When I was busted for shoplifting the last time," she said, "which was my fault—I got too bold, tried to stiff-leg a smoked ham out under my skirt—they sent me to a head doctor, a thought-shaper. He had all sorts of qualifications framed on the wall. He decided my problem was one of nurture, bein' *here*, you know, and asked where would you like to be, and I said, 'Los Angeles.' He said, 'That could be done.' Then I said, 'In 1928.' This got him leaning backwards. 'Now, there's your problem.' And, of course, I already *knew* that."

"Uh-huh. I'd like to be back when the biggest man was fairly small, and I could be a giant."

"Right," she said, and her hand stroked my arm. "Transferred to a period, a rare other time period, when I, *me,* would've been a happy standout, highly esteemed and just crushingly, crushingly special."

"But, here on earth, what're you after?"

Romella's had a strong scent, the smells from various women and their sprays and perm solutions running side by side. Shoe heels clicked on the linoleum floor.

"Better days." She pointed at Jason, who seemed to glow from the attention of his customers. "There's ways and ways to get to those better days; we're going to make use," she said, and waggled her finger toward her brother, "of what we've got. *That right there.* Now you, Sammy, might be able to make sure we get *paid* for using what we've got."

"That sure is an important part of any deal. Any good deal."

"That's why we treat you big, Sammy. That's why we want you in our lives. You make us feel safe—or safer, at least."

Over at the sink I saw Jason wrap a towel around the wet head of this pretty good-lookin' gal, totally adult but fine, and they exchanged quick glances as if things had happened between them during that shampoo that they should try to keep secret.

I realized I was weak to her.

8

Bleed toward the Beach

At night, abandoned house cats roamed the holler, their voices sounding like a pack of babies prowling the tall weeds and trash heaps, wailing for love. They hit notes in their cries that communicated stuff you don't want to understand. They seemed all over out there, and their sounds terrorized Biscuit. He'd hear them and fall to his belly, then shimmy that way across the kitchen floor to the screen door and raise his head just high enough to sneak a peek.

Bev swung by barefoot with a meat lover's pizza one night, and diet pop, and her and Jason and me and Jamalee crowded the kitchen, our presence giving Biscuit enough guts to moan a bit. I sat on a straight-back chair with a dish towel clothespinned around my neck as a barber shawl. Jason had the equipment and needed practice, see, so he dove in on my hair and had at it. He said I'd cut a figure when he was done clipping and buzzing.

"Cut a figure," Bev said. "Right."

I said, "That seems a lot of hair sifting down."

"Be unique," Jason said. "Be aloof and singular."

"Okay. Just, I don't want to be a joke."

"Am I laughing?"

"He's sure not laughing," Bev said. A chair was there for her, crowded in beside the fridge. She dressed to cast her daughter in a frumpy light. Her blond hair had been brushed down and choked into a bun. Her jeans were faded and enticing, snug enough I believe I could see the imprint of her moneymaker. And a black T-shirt.

There was one-butt-wide worth of empty counter space beside the sink, and Jam had hopped up and sat there. The kitchen walls had become the color of baloney rind left in the sun.

She held a road atlas split across her lap.

"This map starts to get really interesting about a state and a half from here."

"Which way?" I asked.

"Every which way, I'd say."

As seemed to be her habit around home, Jamalee wore

an ankle-length and loose smock that covered her shape like a hiding spot she took with her everywhere. The colors, even, were flat: grayish, greenish, whitish. A few times she'd stood with the sun on the revealing side of her and I could see she had a tight tiny figure under there and tended toward little bitty dark panties.

"Why do you think everything away from here is so hot?" I asked.

Bev broke in, like a momma. "It's this way, Sammy. When *I* was a young filly the Beatles showed up in our lives, and all the girls screamed and got soakin' over which ones? Paul and John, of course. But, not *me*." She shook her head and swallowed some pizza. "Huh-uh. I set *my* sights on Ringo, don't you see? If a girl met him, a girl might truly have a chance, him with that nose and all, a chance she'd *never ever* have with Paul or John. My fantasies, don't you see, had *possibility* in them. Now, *Jamalee,* though, she's the sort that has got to have either of the superstar dreamboat Beatles or *both*, or she'll pitch a hissy fit that'll last to her grave."

I said, "Boil *me* down and I'm just a Beatles song. All I need is love, love, love."

"Oh, now, aren't you a sweetie."

"Let me tell you," Jam said, a bit hot, "a story about why."

He had the buzz cutter going along the top of my head, but I turned enough to see her.

"Uh-oh," Jason said, "which one?"

"The school one."

"I think that's maybe your best, hon." Bev dropped a pizza crust back into the box, picked at some stuck cheese. "You've told it the most, anyhow."

"Thank *you*, Beverly. Anyway, Sammy, some years back, when I went to school, I had gotten to be palsy-walsy with this girl, Tabitha Bain, whose family owns the Bain Furniture Factory over there, past—"

The talking got suspended while a train hooted and bullied by, everyone stalling where they were as if a time-out in life had been whistled, until the tracks carried that racket away.

". . . the feed mill."

"Yeah. It's near Happy Bark."

"That's it. Now, the Bains are rich, plenty rich, got the great rich big house up on Penney Drive, starin' down on the town, and Tabitha was just about smart enough to manage a C average if she worked hard. But she was lazy. I mean, she'd been born rich, why bust her hump? But her mother wanted her to go to a hot-shit college someday and land a beau who was at the *national* level of rich, take that next step, you know. So she hired me to do Tabitha's papers for her. Now, every paper I wrote that was handed in with Tabitha's name on them got an A, and my own papers with my own name on them never got higher than a B. Mostly C's. To the teacher, don't you know, a Bain was *supposed* to sail on, but a Merridew should just get pregnant or go to jail or jump off a cliff. The school here had designed *us* for the scrap heap. The heap that hangs out in crummy bars and does minimum-wage spot work." She flipped a page of the atlas. "Our entire futures in West Table had been agreed on and settled the very day we were born." She flipped a few more pages. "That's why *everywhere* else looks good."

Her point was one I'd already felt, but I shared some of the blame in my version. I had been born shoved to the margins of the world, sure, but I had *volunteered* for the pits.

I said, "I hear you, Jam."

Bev pulled a joint rolled in chocolate paper from her cigarette pack and held it beneath her nose. "Everything you told us there could've been turned to your advantage, but no, you'd rather stew and sulk and dream trippy dreams."

"You're not smoking that in here. You know my rules."

"Oh, that's right. No drugs in this house except for those pills you pop, hon."

"I *need* them. They give me tempo."

Jason said, "I don't like arguments. Please stop here."

Bev got up and walked over and pushed out the screen door. "I'm goin' home to have a joint and a highball and turn the TV on to something funny."

She let the door slam.

That boy slaved over my skull. He clipped and studied and buzzed and studied and drug the comb through there.

"You're startin' to really look tough. Are you tough?"

"Me? Tough? Naw, naw, naw. I'm a great big ol' crybaby. You'll see me gettin' rushed to the hospital every time there's a loud noise or a bumblebee threatens me."

She didn't look up from the atlas.

"He's lyin'," she said. "His daddy was a pit bull and his momma was a train wreck."

Then this instrument, a clarinet I thought, started to be played out there in the night. I could hear it clear but that music had traveled to reach me. It seemed to be from atop the ridge above the holler. The song was a kind of ragtime tune, sort of jaunty and limber. The cats took it for the call of a great leader, or something, and bawled their respect.

The kids stared at each other for a tense, long glance; then Jason dropped his implements and basically *lunged* from the kitchen.

I heard the door to his room slam.

I guess my expression asked the question, because she said, "That's Mr. Hart, the music teacher, practicing his dick-sucking on a clarinet. He pulls to the side of that road up there and tosses those musical numbers down here, alluring my brother on."

We both sat there with Biscuit, listening to Mr. Hart unroll his serenade.

"He's got Jason on his mind constantly, I do believe. He's tried to convince Jason that he's Mr. Hart's breed of man."

"Uh-huh."

"He's right, too, but I need Jason to sleep with women."

"How's that?"

"There're all these women calling and everything, offering for Jason to practice on them on Mondays, when Romella's is closed. I need him to woo those ladies so we can get, like, *dues* from them and raise our getaway dough." She retrieved the atlas and opened it to a map of the entire country. She put her finger in the Ozarks where we were. "Palm Beach, Florida. That's the place for us." Her finger moved slow from here toward there. "We get the money, pack up, get a car, and just sort of mosey slow across these other states, just *bleed* toward the beach down there."

I said, "I got a car."

She laughed me into my place and left me there.

For about three or four more songs me and Biscuit sat on the stoop, feeling small together, taking in the music. He was pretty damned good. In fact, that Mr. Hart could *play*!

I kicked the bedroom door open and shouted, "What in the hell did you do to my hair?"

Jason laid on his bunk, belly down. His eyes were red and there were sniffles.

"Oh, don't be mad. It's a style called 'flattop with fenders.' "

"Mad? I *love* it, man! You do truly have a *talent*, kid."

"Don't try to cheer me up."

"I'm not. I *love* what you did here, on my head."

"Don't tell me that if it's not true."

This style of hair said things, made claims. On top it was a flattop, but the sides were long and slicked back to create puffy fenders. It was a hairstyle that'd signify cool cat *rockability*, darlin', if I plucked the upright bass at Hernando's Hideaway in 1956. It was the revealing presentation of that special inner me I'd been looking for, and that boy had found it and gifted it to me.

"Listen, Jason, I'm sincere." I slid my hand across the flat part. "You gave me a trademark. I didn't have one of my own before."

A small wall lamp burned beside his rack. He gave me a couple of looks, looking to see if I was messing with him, then swung around and sat up on the edge of his bunk.

"You'll need some Butch Wax." Jason stood, then, and cocked an eyebrow and sucked on his lips and closely examined my head like he just might bid on it. "Now, that *is* good," he said. "The élan and balance, you know, it's all there."

"Whatever. I like it and thank you, kid, and that's all the thankin' I'm gonna do."

"You're certainly welcome, Sammy, sir."

The light in there was small and vague. Shadows angled and rounded from the corners and the ceiling, and that one puny pat of light sat surrounded by them.

I could see Jason put a hand up to his head, the hand made into a seashell he cupped to an ear. He leaned toward the window where gray moths and brown bugs beat a rhythm against the screen, paused, leaned farther.

"The clarinet," he said. "I don't hear it."

"I think your music friend split."

"*Friend?*" Jason, you know, turned and faced my way, but he was wrapped up in an angled shadow so his expression was kept from me. "That's not the word. That word won't exactly do. I wonder, though, could I talk to you, Sammy? I *need* to talk to *somebody*, and I feel like, you and me, we *are* friends."

He used that word, the word I'd used wrong, but it's the right word to use on me.

I climbed up to my rack and plumped my pillow and stretched out like a mud puddle in a wheel rut.

"What about?"

What I'll say about what Jason said: There had been tumult in his young emotions and recent experiences, and Mr. Hart set off revelations in him and his pecker, and I think Jason knew how he and his pecker truly felt about Mr. Hart, but he needed to be soothed some, patted on the back, told it was okay to go on and be who he was and do those things with Mr. Hart to his true taste again and again, which is a picture I don't care to paint.

Jason finally said, "I felt like he'd wangled and wangled to get me on that field trip. I'd been pretty swept away. You could say I didn't fight as hard as I could've. I can't say it was awful. Ever since then Mr. Hart has been *woo-woo* all over me."

"Think of what you want, kid, what you want to happen or not happen, then make it clear."

"Well, I mean, Sammy, could *you* do it the other way? The sex stuff? The sex stuff with men?"

"They say you can learn to if you draw life."

"What's that answer mean?"

"I ain't drawn life."

Jason, you can see by now, was a really good kid,

basically. I had respect for him and concerns, too. A country queer like that is going to have his interior qualities tested a whole lot. You've got to have a suitcase of respect for such as come through that, and come through it daily—nightly, too, I imagine, and likely the lunch hour as well. It ain't the easiest walk to take amongst your throng of fellow humankind.

"But now, Sammy, my next question to you is, What do you do for heartache?"

That question sprang me from the top bunk to the floor. I wanted to put a finish to this chat.

"Take a switch to it," I said. I let my feet loose. "That's the limit of what I know."

Jamalee hummed in the kitchen, bent inside the fridge, and the fridge light threw a shadow inside her nightie tent that gave me a notion, so I grabbed her ass. That palaver with Jason had got me all stoked for pussy, don't ask me why. Her rump was a firm small melon which my two hands cradled perfect.

She whacked my hands away with hers. She almost turned to look at me, then didn't bother.

"No, no, huh-uh. That's *not* in the cards, Sammy."

"I'm all stoked, Jam. Awful stoked."

"It's not my fault you got yourself a stiffie."

"I really want you, darlin'. Bad."

"Uh-huh, let me guess: You probably already love me, right?"

"That must be it. This feeling."

"Well now, that is *your* downfall, baby. Why don't you take yourself on over next door, here, and visit Bev or something. Visit ol' Bev and get yourself stoned and unwound."

I felt dismissed. She snatched a stalk of celery and moved away, into her nook. She slung the curtain closed fast. Biscuit followed me out the screen door. That mutt sympathized, I'm almost sure. He'd witnessed how she shot me down. His look and posture said he knew how it was, man. Chin up and stuff.

Where the yards weren't scuffed to bare dirt they needed to be cut. The grass grew in tough stranded knots, like forgotten islands if the dirt was sea, and these islands could trip you fast in the dark. Jam had been fairly harsh with me, but her advice seemed sound. Biscuit kept near my heels as I tripped and plunged across the yard.

That mysterioso style of TV light filled Bev's front room. Each new picture on the tube flashed a different variety of light and filled the room with jumpy shadows and a pale glow.

"I see you," she said, before I even knocked. "Let yourself in." Biscuit followed me inside, and she added,

"Did you boys get yourselves *banished* from baby Jamalee's clubhouse?"

"A little," I said.

She sat in a squat soft chair, green, I think, and her feet were up on a stool, or whatever they're officially called, and she wore a pink and cool cotton nightdress and a yellow turban around her hair and her face had a blue face mask on it, shrinking those pores.

"Could I have a beer?"

"If there is any."

There was, and I sat across from Bev in the squeaky rocker. It squeaked whenever you shifted weight and sounded tortured if you actually rocked. It did not enjoy what it had been made to do.

"Need a glass?"

"No."

"Oh, have a glass. I like to see them used."

She went barefoot to the case in the corner and pulled a cocktail glass and handed it to me.

The label said Sloppy Joe's. I poured beer into it, and she sat down and watched me chew through the foam to get at that beer.

"There's a couple of chocolate roaches in that ashtray beside you, Sammy."

Fairly quick after that, the late-night funny boy on the TV got me to laughing. He had a dog on there, a mixed breed that could pull a man's shoes and socks off and hang them in the closet. Funny Boy dug it enough he laid down and had the dog do him, too, and unleashed his funny facial expressions during each blank second. The dog made a big hit as a personal servant.

I couldn't get Biscuit to even watch.

When the next late-night funny-boy show came on, Bev came up out of her chair and said, "I'm sick of seeing that shirt, hon. Don't you have any clothes?"

"Uh. They're bein' held in lieu."

"In lieu?"

"Of rent."

"Ah."

She went somewhere and came back and set a suitcase in front of me. The suitcase was dusty, webby, and creamy tan.

"Open it, Sammy. Those clothes used to belong to Skeets Benvenuti."

"Who's that? That sounds like a gangster."

"Skeets was just a mean sonofabitch, hon, a hustler from Dallas, not truly a gangster." She lit a cigarette with her thin golden lighter and let a funnel of smoke rise before her blue face. "I fell in love with him by accident. I don't believe he did all that much wrong, really, other than, I *heard*, con games and once in a while hurtin' people for fun."

"I ain't takin' *his* clothes."

"Relax. I've been holding them for ten years, hon. Skeets got his money from somewhere I never asked about, but somebody thought they knew, I reckon, and wanted it back. It seems Skeets is no longer with us. That's the indications, anyhow."

I skinned from my dirty shirt and broke into the suitcase. It was mostly shirts and they were mostly button-up grampa-style shirts, with stripes thick enough to be panels or checks of several colors or else exploded across by flowers. The shirts hung on me kind of loose, but that'd be fine with this style of clothes. The pants fit beautiful.

With the haircut and the new duds I was getting to be an interesting figure. Bev had gone off and rinsed her face and now smiled, winked, smiled again at this fresh version of me.

"You know, Bev," I said, and raised my hands tenderly to her shoulders, but she backed away before I finished my soulful pitch.

"Don't bother," she said. "Save it. You're cute and young, and I'm occasionally *agreeable*, but uh-uh." She sat down again. She raised her highball and did away with it. "I've been *too* agreeable. Too agreeable for them to care about."

I kept brushing my hands across my new clothes, and stroking Biscuit, and feeling pretty summery and on the beat. Then the TV ran one of those wee hours call-me-and-jack-off commercials, and a thin moan escaped me. Girls in lingerie lounged on pink silken bedspreads, purring about their phone numbers and your loneliness and how much they'd charge you by the minute to fake they were your special friend whilst you pulled your pud.

Bev laughed and laughed, more or less at me. She raised her feet to the stool, and her legs were no secret up to about mid-thigh. She laughed some more, looking at the poses those girls on the screen slung at me. They easily had me convinced as to what I needed and drooling for it.

"Poor Sammy," Bev said. Her smile worked great, really hung out an invitation. "I *know* you have you some dirty hopes, hon, but I want you to understand that I'm not *encouraging* you when I smile."

9

That'll Make Five

It's around three in the afternoon, or close to it, when Rod drops by. I heard his truck out front, heard the pistons sigh when he killed the engine. A door went *thunk* and I looked outside and he had Biscuit leaping high to lick his face, which had a mustache, the bandito style.

Rod wore a T-shirt that claimed him for REO Speedwagon. He displayed the exact look of Classic Rock: large showy belt buckle, tight torn jeans, long black hair hanging from the spots where he hadn't gone bald. You looked at him and you could just almost hear bigheaded guitar riffs and a cheesy drum solo and an FM disc jockey waxing heavy about those olden times.

"Who're you?"

"I'm Sammy. I been stayin' here."

"Are you in the air force, army, one of those?"

"Naw."

"That haircut."

"It's fresh—just got it."

"Jason?"

"I really like it."

"Good. Good."

His truck was a pickup, a Dodge that'd been thumped around plenty and not washed much. The color used to be yellow but had gotten to be adorned with a patch-work of black and gray primer sprayed over repair spots. A large orange ice chest and some rusty logging chains lay in the bed.

"Now, who the fuck are you again?"

Rod had been called home by a legal problem. He had ninety days reserved for him in the Howl County Jail.

Him, me, Jam, Jason sat around in the kitchen, me and him knocking down a jug of bourbon and a twelve-pack of brew. Rod figured to dive drunk into the time he had to do, which began after supper.

Once he heard I was from Arkansas we started to trade jokes to each other, all those wheezing old jokes based on what state you came from, except I told them on my own state and Rod did the same. It got to be like we had a contest to see who could run their home state down the furthest the fastest.

"Then the Missourian says, 'It ain't the mule's legs that's too long, it's his ears.' "

"She says, 'Doctor, I can't seem to use the Pill; every time I stand up, it just falls right back out.' "

"Then the Missourian studies the scrawl of yellow snow and says, 'Don't you think I recognize my own daughter's handwriting?' "

"He says, 'I've got a case of diarrhea,' and the other old Arkansawyer says, 'Well, put it on ice, I'll be over to help you drink it later.' "

"It wasn't his legs was too long, it was . . ."

We killed time talking that way, testing each other, adding the refreshments to our bloodstreams. Jamalee and Jason hardly said a word except about the welfare checks, the weather, the problem in the bathroom plumbing and so forth. They only barely tolerated Rod in his own house.

"I'll leave my truck parked here," Rod said, at about the time when the evening TV news comes on. "Since it's my place and all." He fell sideways from his chair, grabbed my shoulder, pulled me toward the door. "There's somethin' I need to show you, bud."

He took me to his truck. Biscuit slept underneath in

the shade behind a tire. That evening heat hung around and made sure nobody enjoyed the outdoors too much. Some old boy across the road and down a few houses kept up a racket trying to cut the grass of his entire yard with a Weedwacker. He stopped and dragged an ice chest along behind him after every five or six paces of whacking. His woman stood on the porch glaring with two crumb snatchers trying to shinny up her legs. He drank fast in the heat and tossed the empties into the road and dragged that ice chest and made his noise.

"I need you to hold this." Rod pulled a pistol from his truck. "It might get ripped off if I left it here and shoot some sonofabitch and get me blamed. My luck can run that way."

The pistol shined like a Shreveport pimp's favorite teeth. The fine print on the barrel said OLIVETTI FIREARMS and claimed the caliber was thirty-eight though it had a shape I think of as a forty-five. He had one box of bullets. There's a song I know that says a pistol is the Devil's right hand. In my hand it's oiled, loaded, and in my head it's already nagging.

"Where do I put it?"

"Fuck do I care? Just keep it, that's all."

We got to the door and he says, "Now, you ain't goin' to go robbin' silly places, are you? You look like you'd stick up a Chinese laundry just for the conversation."

"Naw, they barely ever say anything."

"I know it. Lord knows I know it."

Rod wouldn't eat, but I had a can of beans with a hot dog sliced into it. I acted responsible and switched to beer only. There was butter bread to sop around in the bean juice. Jamalee and Jason thought Rod and me were plastered and went away from our fumes and kept away.

Rod said, "I never did get nowhere with her."

"Who's that?"

"Jamalee. I never did get to see if that li'l girl's cuffs matched her collar or they didn't. Not even close."

"She's got standards."

"She's got a cob up her ass, is what she's got. Her hair used to be a normal color, too. Brown, I think. And that Jason, Jesus Christ, my old lady always went on and on like a fuckin' groupie over how handsome that faggot was. How his eyes was liquid and deep, or some shit of that sort."

"He *is* pretty damn cute."

"If his nose was broke a couple of times he'd be a better man. Some sort of man. I thought about helpin' him that way a few times, too, when my bitch kept sayin', 'Jason Merridew is the prettiest boy in the total Ozarks, and the prettiest *person*, period, in town, here.' "

"You can't hold that against *him*."

"Nope. I whipped *her* ass, though. Bitch talkin' about another man that way, right before my face. '*He's so pretty.'* She left me not long after, took my kids from me, but I reckon I made my point. I reckon she feels my point yet, wherever she's got to."

He gave me a warning in my black Ford. I had to drive him to the jail. He said, "Beverly—you know, I ain't tellin' tales out of school, bud—but she snitched on some fellas, once I know of for sure. I wouldn't care to be lyin' next to her in bed if them or their friends come callin'. They're vicious, vicious tush hogs, man—Timlinson's from Shannon County. They posed as state cops, a few years back, and robbed pot growers all around here, and folks say they shot two or three poor fuckers. Dead. Shot them dead. Bev fucked 'em, then dropped a dime."

I didn't say a word.

That could easy have been me involved.

I didn't trust my voice.

"Just thought I'd say so, in case you wanted to know."

The jail sat way over at the other edge of town. It was a new one, bigger than you'd figure was needed, made of big slabs of concrete curried to look like stone, with long thin windows up high and bright lights.

I drove the way I was convinced I would if I hadn't drunk three or four shots of bourbon and a few beers. I held my head straight with concentration.

"This is my fourth drunk drivin'," Rod said as I pulled over. He said it with a shrug and a smile, as if this meant he was a real sport, a party-animal fun junkie. "If they catch me the night of the day I get out . . ."

"That'll make five," I said. "I read you clear."

10

Spared the Expectation

Which is the proper response to a written invitation? When introducing couples what name is given first, the gal's or the dude's? When does a man take his hat off, and why is he wearin' one anyhow? What is the usual hour of the day to start passing the jug around at an informal wine-tasting party? Does shrimp cocktail call for this fork or that fork or some other goofy utensil you never heard of and wouldn't recognize if the First Lady stabbed it into the back of your fuckin' hand?

Jamalee had acquired a great thick dilapidated and somewhat dampened book of manners, and the book smelled like a cotton picker's hatband. She spotted lessons in that volume and tossed them before us, and we three snuffled after the kernel of meaning. The main idea was that we should each of us shed the skin that limited us, the social costumery we wore that communicated our low-life heritage at a glance, and adopt a new carriage and a routine of manners and that air of natural-born worthiness that the naturally born worthy displayed.

"We weren't raised with decent values," she said. "We'll have to memorize some on our own."

Jamalee needed to borrow a desert of hot sand and scour it through our skulls so we could start over with scrubbed-clean skulls and build uncrippled brains to stock anew with useful thoughts and habits and intentions.

This process went on over a span of days.

Jamalee would bow her tomato head, dive into the warped pages of that book, then trot out more protocol you couldn't imagine ever needing to know. She was teachy around many themes: learn this, taste this, become that different thing. She wanted us to become "civilized," which I think to her meant to ape the quality folks right down to spittin' at our own shadows.

The radio was kept tuned to the classical station, and I don't care much for any music you'd go crazy if you tried to hum. I'd sit there agitated by the Great Foreign Masters and listen to her just enough to avoid arguments. Fairly often she'd use the book as a guide to construct place settings for a formal dinner, only without the right silverware or dishes, then run us over the whole course and chastise our imaginations if we mistook the white plastic knife for the consommé spoon.

At times Jason would get weary and impatient and she'd say, "Hey, I'm not doing this trying to torture you."

"You don't have to try," he'd say. "I'm *easily* tortured."

Usually we'd be in the yard as the month of May slid by, or in the kitchen, and that tiny hard-nosed girl worked away at us. She was my junior in years but probably three times smarter and older in every useful way. She'd come to solutions where I'd yet to note there was a question.

"Then," she said eventually, "we must master the proper mode of treatment for, as it says, Those Who Are in Our Service. This is crucial, because the high and mighty judge the other high and mighty by how they treat their peons, dig?"

The girl put bubbles in my spirit with her dedication and hope. She tried to speak with curlicues in her language, fancy twists in her high-blown sentences. She usually leaned into whatever she said, worked it over in her head before letting it fly, so the words she'd come out with would help her seem to be that other person, not the one she was but the one she was in training to become.

The world she aimed us at seemed like a child's wish of

a world, except, okay, for the male prostitution and the blackmail.

I, myself, often wished to be spared the expectation of better days ahead or such. On my own it basically never came up.

It was said to me twice by Jamalee that Bev's motto went, "Live fast, learn slow." Once this motto had been quoted when we watched Bev spill from a Lincoln and stagger inside with *two* lovey-dovey paychecks in short-sleeve white shirts and fat neckties. Another time the motto came up when Bev fell by with a sack of burgers and shakes but had forgotten to get Jam's built with no mustard or pickles. Jam flung the motto in Bev's face and Bev just laughed back at her.

"You've got freedom of choice, hon. Your choice could be to go hungry. I sure do want you to suit yourself."

On those off nights, nights when I knew Bev sat over there living fast and learning slow alone, I'd drift by sometime after dark-thirty and visit with her. Biscuit served as chaperone. A beer could generally be found there, and a doobie or two, and a bag of chips, maybe. Cigarettes are the one common vice I never did bond with, but now and again I'd bum a menthol from her and give that bad habit I lacked another chance to take hold. She always was easy to be around. Most often she'd be in a simple shift or a thin robe, and lots of times she had beauty gunks applied to her face. Her hair would either be strapped up by a turban or hanging down plain. As to shoes she was partial to a casual barefoot state instead.

It was in a way a bit like a factory locker room after a twelve-hour shift. Bev kept her feet raised up and her mind kicked back. We watched a lot of funny-boy shows, and endless car-wax infomercials, and sitcoms from her childhood on that channel that shows nothing else.

If I introduced any interesting subjects she mostly waved them away.

"Sammy, your company is fine, and you're welcome enough. I'd rather *not* drink alone. But I'm telling you for the umpteenth time—don't ask me about my *day*. Don't tell me about yours, either. Don't go *prying* into my history, which is *not* open to you. Drink a beer, huh? *In*-hale. Lay back and unwind, watch TV, and when you see a chance of it, go on and laugh. *That's* what we're here for."

One time I asked who Jam's daddy might be.

She answered, "What's past is past. I don't care to sit around and stare back at it."

"Bev, don't you have *any* regrets?"

"Of course I do."

"Like what?"

She turned and flicked a sharp glance at me.

"Like I should've went blond younger. I *regret* that I didn't."

"Geez, you sure are Madam Hardboiled, ain't you?"

"Sammy, I do believe you've been *practicing* my motto."

The music came with dark and I went after it. I had to drive toward the square then backtrack in half a circle to reach the ridge above the holler. I pushed in a tape of "Monkey Beat" and twisted the volume high and frisky. The drive took four or five minutes to arrive two hundred yards above where I'd started.

I slid in beside Mr. Hart's wheels. This spot was a narrow overlook with a gray safety rail and a thinly graveled parking area. He drove a nice lime pickup truck, a Chevy from about 1970 or so, the best-looking truck era. I stayed in the Pinto until "Rockin' Dog" raised my spirits and finished, then got out and went toward the clarinet.

I stepped over the gray guardrail and went down through a steep patch of woods toward the music. I sort of expected an audience to be sitting there, maybe drinking hot tea from thin brittle china cups, watching Mr. Hart's fingers skitter over the clarinet, but there was only Mr. Hart, perched on a dead tree fallen lengthwise. He seemed to be wearing his gym clothes, basically. His hair was dark and longish and fell limp around his face. The instrument case lay open at his feet.

He saw me but finished the song, which damned if I know what it was, but it sounded like a Bugs Bunny soundtrack, before he said, "May I help you?"

"You keep droppin' music down on Jason Merridew, man, and, like, what are your intentions, anyhow?"

"Who are you?"

"Let's say I'm family."

He bends over, then, and puts the clarinet in the case and latches it. He set the case on the log beside him.

"I've *met* his family. You're not in it, as far as I know."

"Let's say I'm the part of the family you *don't* know. So, answer me what you're up to, man, or maybe I'll have to beat your ass. Hear?"

I could see he smiled at that.

I could see he stood up, and smiled again, too.

"With your fists? *You* think you're going to beat *me* with your fists?"

"Or, if you make me, could be I'll shoot your ass."

"I don't see a gun. Do you have a gun in your car? You look like somebody who might, but, I don't know, do you?"

His attitude was getting interesting, so I looked on him a bit closer. He stood a nip shorter than me but was a double-hand-span wider. He wore a convincing smile that was relaxed and said he'd been here before and the memories weren't all bad, I guess. I took note for the first time that he was one of those iron-pumping queers, which nobody had warned me about, arms big enough to square-dance upside down on. He probably was raised wrestling steers and playing fullback, one of those.

"All right, looky here. *Forget* the part about beatin' your ass. Just *forget* that phrase. That wasn't right of me to say. I *still* need to know what you're up to."

"I'll tell *him* that when next I see him."

"Well, his sister's gettin' anxious down there."

Mr. Hart picked up the clarinet case and snagged it under an arm. We both started uphill, to the parking area.

"He's been avoiding me."

"He's confused."

"I know he likes me, but—"

"He's confused, man, let's let it lay right there, too, okay?"

We stood beside his truck, which was perfect, inside and out. A couple of cars rolled by and striped us with their headlights.

"You came on like such a bully," he said. "You misjudged. That doesn't work on me."

"I'm just concerned. But I do sort of think he's, you know, a little *young* for a goat your age."

"What does he think?"

"I told you, he's in a muddle on this."

"I'll be patient."

"Well, your music ain't doin' on Jason exactly what it is you want it to do, man."

He got in his truck, behind the wheel. That engine purred, sounded stroked, petted, doted on, ageless.

"So you think you *know* what I want."

I said, "I know what you want *eventually*. That part I don't expect is any mystery, Mr. Hart."

His retort was that he drove away.

By day I tried to slave-drive myself back into physical shape. Rod had a rusty old weight bench and a stack of weights, so I dragged it all outside under the tree in the side yard. For me to be truly useful as a goon involved in blackmail I needed to inflate my muscles just a tad. I didn't have any fat on me, but that was mostly due to a recent crank hobby and not very regular mealtimes. I laid on the bench in the heated shade and grunted and heaved and sweated like a beer bottle at a church picnic.

A few times Jason became intrigued and joined in. He'd grunt along with me and break a comely sweat, then go sit at Jamalee's side on the stoop and look gorgeous. I'd have my shirt off and he'd be sitting there studying on me as if he knew someday he'd have to describe me to a police sketch artist. His gaze lounged and lingered on my bare chest and, truth to tell, I'd be driven squirmy by it.

"Jason, damn it, will you stop starin'?"

"Was I staring, Sammy, sir?"

"Like a robin at a worm."

"My mind wandered," he said. "I was sitting here, thinking about *Eng*-land."

"Well, face the other way and think about England, huh?"

During that spell we lived a nutty life. I was getting my rights and wrongs from Jamalee's head. Two and two was makin' five, sexual blackmail of rich horny women was merely a career option, and the future figured to be a swank banquet spread in our honor, with dwarves for waiters and lambs on spits.

It felt crazy, but so what?

Everybody among us on earth has their own cherished horsefeathers that they try and try and try to believe in.

II

~

Whoop

I could see a John Law focus on the ass end of my Pinto when I drove us past him into the parking lot. He sat comfy in his air-conditioned cop car watching for sweaty citizens he could make sweat extra. This occurred at the Willis and Oates grocery store on the near side of town, and the lot that stretched wide had the color of oil. Quite a number of vehicles parked there, a big percentage belonging to folks at a wedding in the church across the street.

"We" entailed Bev and me and Jamalee, and we came after some special smoked bacon for Jason's favorite meal. It apparently involved noodles and garlic and sprinkle cheese as accomplices, but wasn't all it could be without that special bacon as ringleader. This store was the store that carried it.

We got out and stood on that dark lot, and you could feel the hot pavement through the soles of your boots. All three of us made weary sounds. The mean part of July had bum-rushed town early, in the final week of May, and was souring plans everywhere it went. I've known Easters that were close on to one hundred degrees, so you can't predict the weather too fine in this part of the map.

I allowed myself a phony li'l cough and shot a glance at John Law. He wore shades, but I know his eyes were entirely on me.

"Let's split up," Jam said. "I'm looking for some items for me, also."

"Now, don't you—," Bev started, but Jam waved her quiet before she spoke any farther.

This clerk started to stalk me as soon as I came inside the store. I had on a clean tropical shirt, and I'd shaved and all, but there's a flavor to my scent that acts as an early warning, I suppose. He wore a butcher's bib and khaki pants, and he was down in age yet, down in age to where his face skin still erupted ugly on him. Every aisle I turned up interested him, too. I inspected the labels on canned goods, got to almost be able to pronounce the more scientific ingredients, then lifted melons and thumped them and so forth like somebody with purchasing power. He just stood there constantly in the corner of my eye. I reckon he was hoping I'd spot him and recognize his serious intentions and not pull anything so he wouldn't be forced to discover if he truly *could* handle a dude of my ilk, or would he toss up his hands and run. I lingered inside the lines of the law, though, and let the fella go on preaching to himself about how he surely would have slapped me silly if I'd made a desperate gangster move on so much as a licorice stick.

I linked up with Jamalee and Bev in the meat lane, and in my eye corner that clerk called forth a disgusted look and smeared it on his face. It would seem he knew them and knew their story.

"This store," Jam said, "gets on my nerves." She looked toward this older gal in a pale green clerk's smock who chewed gum and leaned against a freezer staring toward the ceiling like she saw a weeping Jesus there invisible to all others. "They almost don't allow you to shop, hanging over your shoulder all the time."

"You're lucky they still let you in, hon."

"I'm not lucky about nothin'."

"Just let the cool air cool you," Bev said. She fluffed her hair loose and shook. The temperature influenced her nipples in a kindly direction. "This cool air works real good on me."

"Don't get used to it, 'cause we can't take it on home with us."

"Nope," I said. "Sack won't hold it."

At the head of the aisle my stalker and her stalker appeared to be sharing war stories. I could see Jamalee did not care for this sort of treatment, hated it from her bones out, and just might run her tiny self up the aisle, there, and let her itty-bitty fists fly. At certain angles she sure enough did *look* like an Irish flyweight, a snappy li'l fighter with the most tomato-red hair in County Malarkey and a strangely cute face.

"Might be we should go outside," I said. "Wait at the car."

Bev said, "Might be you should. I can hunt the bacon. Let's see if we can get all the way home, though, without any *warrants* bein' sworn out, huh?"

"*All* the way?" Jam said.

"Yeah," I said, "don't set the pole *too* high for us, Bev."

She swooped a hand to my face and had a pinch of my cheek. She was smiling, and I recognized that, with a month on a cottage cheese and pineapple diet, or the grapefruit one, or one such as them, she'd be up there around the mighty-damn-fetching level of looks, just a beauty mark and fattened lips shy of drop-dead gorgeous, for her age.

We moved and she moved.

The stalkers paused in their chitchat as Jam and me walked up the aisle. My stalker, I think, was overpraising himself inside the packed auditorium in his head, taking tall fancy credit for deterring savage me from, I imagine, robbing and raping all through the frozen food section. The applause he was hearing was probably loud and gushy.

"These shop clerks," Jam said, looking right at them. "Their attitude to me is, like, 'You stink. Please come again.' "

"They followed me, too."

"Well, yeah, but anybody *would* you."

"I've forgot that once or twice."

Our stalkers were dishing out some sour and insulting expressions to us. Mine got squirrelier the closer I got to his face skin and the pus pebbles displayed there, and I executed a pause upon reaching him and gave him some free advice: "Time comes when you attain sex with an actual woman that skin'll start to clear up, hoss. Now hand jobs won't do the same, but I don't need to tell that to you, do I?"

He didn't muster a response with me at sucker punch range, except his eyes pulsed more open for a second, but his fellow stalker got pink and openmouthed and turned her gray head away from him in sympathy or contempt or one of those feelings.

Tomato Red appreciated my gesture and put her hand in mine, then thought better of it and yanked loose.

Whatever.

I can't say that yank didn't sting.

At the car I plugged in a homemade music tape, stuff from off the radio in Memphis, and it was mostly Dale Hawkins and Billy Lee Riley and Link Wray and Charlie Feathers, Founding Father rockabilly, which is the music that is my anthem. I got to toe tappin' and hip swayin' in my seat, and sweat gurgled out from inside me, and even Jamalee bobbed along in tune at times.

I had parked facing the church. The church was bright white and pointed and seemed like a structure that would rough me up with scolds and lectures and ghastly passages from the Book if ever I walked on that side of the street. The church steps were crowded. There was a barrage of tuxedos and taffeta and happy hopeful mugs.

The good world, regular happy life; I never had no hand in that, so it's interesting for me to watch it. They seem so sure of their road and what they'll pass by along the way and what they'll find at the end.

Me, I couldn't stand to know that much about what's ahead. I expect I'd be crippled by the fright.

So Jam and me sat there listening to rockabilly and watching the church like they'd devised a stage show to amuse us, and then came the whoop.

The colored lights caught my eye in the rearview mirror, so I doused the music and sat up straight. When it's full-on the noise from John Law is *whoop-whoop-whoop-whoop*, but the man this time just tapped the siren for a lone *whoop*.

I sat still in the car the way they want.

"Shit," Jam said. "You don't have any dope in here, I hope."

My plates should run clean.

"No. There might be a couple of roaches somewhere."

She had a hand held over her eyes and her head drooped.

"We've got to get our plan in gear. It has to happen— I'm so sick of this."

When you look as if you are a person who should in any circumstances be considered a suspect, you get put through the drill plenty. Big boss man comes sidling up on the driver's side, hand on his pistol butt, stayin' just over my shoulder for a clear shot in case I might *snap* and want to blast my way free of a parking ticket. John Law has standard demands: license, registration, name of passenger. He runs the paperwork through the behemoth computer they've got that keeps track of us un-mainstreamed residents till the day the rulers decide to stack us all in a pile and squash us like little irritants. The computer keeps us easy to find. On me the computer prints out that I'm temporarily clean, with no outstanding warrants and no more tail on my parole, either. Yet damned if I don't *smell* guilty.

He hands my papers back and says, "There you go, Mr. Barlach." He says my name wrong, then leans to my window. He smells of baby powder and Old Spice and has a mint clicking behind his teeth so he's got sweet breath and is prepared to start kissin' at any second. He says, "You and your vehicle match a description."

"What's that, cool cat in car? Is that the description?"

"Is that your tuxedo on the backseat, Mr. Barlach? See, the description was of a redneck with no shirt in a tuxedo jacket punching people's mouths over in the East Main Trailer Court a month back. And this vehicle is the brand he drove away in. Also, now, a tuxedo—wouldn't you know it?—is one of the items missin' after a break-in at the McCubbin place on that *same* night. Why don't you both step out of that car for me."

I used my teeth to clamp my lips shut.

His face was blank space.

"Hands on the trunk," he said. "You know the position—feet back and spread."

"Hey, now," Jam said, and she sounded pissed, "this metal is too fuckin' hot." It was, too, and she took her hands away and he shoved her back. "It's burning me!"

96

"I don't care, ma'am. You move again and I'll lock your ass up."

"You don't need to shove her, moth—"

"Don't say it," he said. "That's the word that'll turn this ugly, boy."

We're in the search position, hands on trunk, facing the church, and this clearly with child gal in a bridal gown and a fella who everybody probably knows someone who he looks like come floating from the mouth of the church, and flung rice makes a small personal blizzard in the air and garters take off in it and fall to the ground. A few folks in the crowd are noticing our minor drama, but not enough to stall the happy cheers.

"Mr. Barlach, do I have your permission to search your vehicle?"

This has become a trick question, because there's no way to answer it and no use trying. You can say yes, and be searched without good reason, or say no and be made to stand in the hot sun till a warrant arrives, and judges hand these sorts of warrants out as though they were snapshots of their grandkids. *Then* you get searched. The high courts have said John Law can now legally do dang near anything he wants with you and your property any *time* he wants. If he turns up a roach, your car might have a new berth in his driveway.

"Be my guest," I said, "but don't make a mess."

It's no use to squawk against these wrong laws—they've already won, baby, whether you slept through it or not.

The man begins to root for grubs in my car.

I saw the wedding bouquet in the air and saw this look of fear, sort of, on the face of the girl who caught it. She wore a little crown of flowers. She seemed only about thirteen, mostly long legs and knee knobs, but made a good catch.

Jam's got her head hung low and is moaning and has steam shootin' from her ears. When she spoke she sounded like she might break down bawling.

"God damn," she says, "you know, that big rotten gap between who I am, and who I want to be, never does quit *hurtin'* to stare across."

"Well, hell," I said, feeling the Pinto wiggle as the cop rooted around, "that's what dope is for."

"Ah, if I was only stupid, it wouldn't be so hard."

"Shit, Jam, everybody who *ain't* stupid has thought that thought, then been as stupid as they need to be for a spurt, then changed their minds back later."

"Here comes the bacon with Bev carrying it."

Bev ambles along, holding the bacon in a sack, and shows she's got skills unimagined. She looks into my car, peers at John Law, then says, "William? . . . William, what's the trouble here?"

William backs out of the car, holding the tuxedo jacket. He comes across sort of pleased to see Bev but not so pleased that I see he's pleased. That variety of moment.

"Well, hey, Bev."

"Hey to you too, William. What's going on?"

"Are these your people?"

"Depends on what they've done."

"Nothin' I'm sure of." He then held the tuxedo jacket up and let the sun beat on it. Mildew had attached to some sections and laid a faint green icing down the sleeves. "I'd like to know where this here came from."

"You don't know?" Bev barreled into him with her smile. "That's ol' Skeets Benvenuti's clothes—you recall him?"

"*Skeets?* Oh, hell, yes."

"All that boy's clothes came from Skeets's ol' suitcase. He was a careful dresser, you know?"

"Pretty sharp, all right." He got a removed quality to his face for a snap of time, lost in a quick look backwards, I guess. "Skeets. Skeets. Is he dead, or what?"

"He never was as live as you are, William."

"I always hated to arrest him. He was that fine of a guy, a li'l quick-tempered but great to have a few pops with, out at the Inca Club."

Jam and me both pulled our hands from that scorching trunk and blew on them.

"Yeah," Bev said. "Skeets was a mighty charming piece

of shit when he wasn't takin' advantage of you." She sprung her hips into a certain stance and showed a glow to her skin and smile and blond hair in the sunbeams. "Too bad somebody disappeared him."

William tossed the jacket back into my car, then wiped his hands together. He spit twice, then began to nod at Bev.

He said, "I expect the world has gone on a lot better without Skeets than he ever did believe it could. He thought everything'd fly off-kilter without him. He thought he was that necessary, and entitled to certain privileges because he was."

Bev tilted her head to the side and let her feet slide a little farther apart.

"You knew Skeets better'n I ever knew you did."

The man had no smile now. He stared over at the wedding and had his hands hooked into his pistol belt.

"There's been several silly break-ins at nice homes in recent months, and that's got to stop. Not much has been stolen yet. Somebody'll pay steep next time. Get your people home, Bev. It's been nice to see you. To see you again, I mean."

The car felt like a cookie oven. Jam was sort of upset at the roust by the law, and even more by the fact that Bev could fix the trouble. Jam griped plenty.

Bev sat in the back but leaned forward. She said, "Hon, you don't confront trouble. You *flatter* it."

The trees alongside the roads had gotten smug in the heat and stingy with their shade. The breeze had made a side deal with the trees to not blow, either, driving way up the value of shade.

"It's not fuckin' fair," Jam said.

"*Fair?*" Bev said. "Poor baby. Look, you're really sayin' that the ways of life are glum and grim and nasty, and I guess you want to turn crybaby about that, but what's on *my* mind is, Whoever misled you things were otherwise, hon? What sugar factory spun *you* out with such silly candy-assed notions? For cryin' out loud. There's other staples I'll break to you right now, too: The sun gives life but you'd be an ash flake if you got close to it, you got to swallow water to live but sometimes it kills you, Uncle Sam don't *truly* count you as any relation, and God has gone blank on your name *and* face.

"Whew! Now, then, let's have a beverage and a belly laugh and get on with living forward, huh?"

Jam sat there, deeply sulky. She could make her mood smother yours.

I put in, "Plus, love is a can of worms."

The car hadn't come to a stop in the drive when Jam shoved out and left the door yawning. I shut the Ford down and said, "She's in a state."

"Uh-huh."

I pulled the seat forward so Bev could climb out the passenger door. She put her hand over mine. When I looked at her she looked back, and looked back electric and steady.

"Sammy, did you jack off thinkin' about me last night?"

"Uh, no."

"You *didn't*? It *felt* like maybe you did."

"I did jack off. I ain't denyin' *that*."

Her nose wiggled fast as a wink and was chased by a grin.

"I believe you just *answered* my question, hon. It was sweet of you."

12

So-so Desire

Then came a Monday.

I knew it wouldn't go well, but it went even worse.

"I can't find my feeling for this. I have to *think, think, think* before every move." Jason had his flabbergasted beautiful face in the pooched-out part of the screen-door screen, whispering to Jam and me. We both sat to the side of the stoop like trash cans, but he took our advice whenever he slunk to the screen and could hear us. "I don't flow at this. I don't flow at this at all."

The woman's car sat in the drive, and it was a glistening blue boat of a car, a Caddy, and its presence in our dirt-rut drive asked the question, What's wrong with this picture? The woman had gone into the powder room, but not to powder from the sounds of it. She'd had a shampoo, a set, a manicure, and had gotten so flirty toward Jason with her words and tone and squeezing fingers that he'd started to freak.

I whispered, "Put your hand on her thigh."

"Then what?"

"Uh, well, slide your hand up under her skirt, there, and say, 'How 'bout I take your temperature, ma'am?'"

"*What?*"

Jamalee shoved me and made a sound of pity.

"That's awful, Sammy. That's pitiful. That might work on the pigs you've gone with but, huh-uh, not with this gal."

"What then?" There were beads of sweat in his voice. "And give it to me quick. I hear the toilet paper rolling."

"Jason," I said, "don't do anything except respond. All you've got to do is stand still, *don't run,* and give her a smile or two. Believe me, she'll ransack you on her own any minute now—she's probably in the john puttin' her thing in."

"Her wh—?"

The woman wore heels that took charge as she walked, went *snap snap snap* across the floor. Her smell reached out to me—outside, there, even, on the dirt—and it did the job. That smell set a mood, set a mood so I wanted to sprint in there and tell Jason to scamper his fabulous skinny ass out of the way and let the *big dog* eat.

His face through the screen expressed doom.

He turned to face the footsteps.

"Now, Mrs. Mallahan, perhaps I should practice my head-and-neck massage. Would you care for a cup of tea first?"

"What I'd care for, tiger, is if you'd call me Linda, as I keep askin'."

"Okay, Linda. I have herbal tea or regular-tea tea."

"Sit by me on the couch, there, tiger, and explain herbal flavors to me. I'm a bourbon person, most often. You, pretty fella, are takin' me to new places."

"You sure you want me to—uh, you know, sit by you? Linda?"

Those footsteps started snapping.

"Did I sound like I was confused about what I want?"

He started to follow.

"Not too much."

He was, I think, guessin' every inch of the way. Jason, I'm sure, hadn't had any pussy since pussy had him. He's on the couch, there, pretty quick, *guessing* his way toward her fulfillment, throwing every guess he's got at the woman, and he only had one guess or two in his bag to start with. All he had to offer her was his beauty and that so-so desire.

Me and Jamalee are anxious lumps beside the stoop, at the ready to give coaching instructions during any time-outs. Our spot is under the porch rail. There are bugs under there, cobwebs and fallen wasp combs, and old sharp-edged bottle tops you discover suddenly with your butt.

"Did you ever even ask that boy if he *could* fuck a woman?"

"I don't *ask* questions I don't want to hear the answer of."

The sky had turned ash gray and greasy with sweat, like a heart attack was coming up from the south. The dirt smelled inviting. The sounds from the couch carried through the tiny shack and sifted out the screen door, down to us where we squatted.

"It's never just life," Jamalee said. As she listened to her brother and the woman, her posture became one of low tide, drained and slack. "It's always a tired-ass *lesson* from life."

Doors had been slammed shut in the dream house.

The three of us moped in the kitchen, Jamalee chewing her lips and Jason drying his eyes, trying to breathe slow and wipe the red from his face.

He said, "I *knew* it. I *knew* it would be like *that*."

"Come on," I said. "It's not *all* bad."

"I'll *never* be normal now."

"Kid, you weren't *ever* goin' to be normal. Not you. Normal belongs to other folks."

A passing train cast its spell, put us on hold where we stood, took time from our lives and ate it. The spell was long, loud, welcome.

Jason dunked his head in the sink again, washing his face for the eighty-seventh time or close to it. That woman had worked the boy like a rented mule that hated the work and kept trying to run toward open pasture and had to be reined in hard and bossed.

At the end she'd giggled and giggled and called him "Dear child."

It didn't occur to her, apparently, to leave him a wad of cash.

"I suppose what we'll do," Jamalee said, "is we'll just the three of us have us a nice sad pity party. We'll cower here, shiver and shake, and share stories about our weaknesses. All the lame things about us that make us *pointless*. Which we are, we're *pointless*."

"Now listen," Jason said. His voice ran high on him. "If *you* want, Sis, we can be totally honest about *you*— *brutally* honest, even—but I'd very much prefer it if we'd keep *sugar-coating* anything said about *me*. Is that so much to expect?"

Beyond the screen door I spotted this snake. A milk snake, I'd say. It came into view from near where we'd squatted as trash cans. The snake went by slow and unconcerned, as if it thought it was playing a round of golf or something. I saw it ripple toward a grass knot and suddenly it was gone, totally gone, as if it had never been there, like a truth you didn't tell.

In a short time it became only me and Jamalee standing there. She had half circles of dirt dusted on her smock where her squatting butt had met the dirt. Dust moons as a designer's touch. They drew my eyes.

"I'll need a job," Tomato Red said. "My brother won't do at all as a stud."

"I had my doubts," I said. I raised my hands to my flattop, then rubbed the fenders. "But he's got these other talents."

"So, I'll get a job, raise the money that way. I can get a job, how about you?"

"They'll have to hang me first. Then I'll hunt up some sort of grunt work. Grunt work is my main calling, but I like to be dead when I do it."

"Aw, shit, Sammy, that future sounds awful." This was a sorry day for baby Jam, the day the transmission fell plumb out of her plan. It left her skittery and raw and wondering. "It's not right."

"Ah," I said, "we *are* havin' one."

"One what?"

"Pity party. Like you said: *my* lifelong boo-hoos, *your* lifelong boo-hoos; we'll celebrate them, talk them out into the complete wide open."

Oh, now Jamalee did *not* care for my comment. She gave me a look that suggested she just might dismiss gravity or some such until I learned my fuckin' place. I won't claim she managed to do that, but if I did it'd certainly make a fresh excuse for me. No?

13

Fuss and Feathers

You weren't born choking on no silver spoon, you know how it goes when you go looking for a job and you need one: You wait in the first indifferent room, ink in the forms, apply in another room with linoleum that's waxy and squeaks and overhead lights that don't miss a thing; then there's the desk and the person behind it who thinks he's an admiral, or it's a she and she thinks she's now in line for the throne to somewhere, and next you're kissing ass and aw-shucsing toward the desk, telling how bad all your life you've been wanting to be night janitor in a chemical plant, or hog wrangler in a slaughterhouse, or pizza delivery boy, how you've laid awake in bed gettin' goose bumps just from *imagining* how high and wide your life might someday be lived if ever you *could* average five dollars and forty cents an hour.

But there're these questions, as always: Could you explain what you did from February of that one year until July of the next? And also that other year, from May to September?

Oh, did I not write that down? you say, then start spinning phantom jobs out your mouth, and they're the best you ever did have, too: roller-coaster operator at Six Flags; Delta guide and driver for that two-part *National Geographic* article; day bartender at Silky O'Sullivan's.

Your palms break sweat and you sit there, needy, while your work ethic and character are available for comment from strangers you wouldn't share a joint with at a blues festival.

And you don't get the job.

Those old failings showed through.

Not even lies helped.

Before all that long, you start telling those near to you that you went on interviews that turned out sorry when factually you never even made the phone call.

Jamalee dwindled out of hope in a few days longer than I'd taken to dwindle. We sat in the kitchen quite a bit after that and let the heat kick our asses so we didn't have to do it. I worked on the remains of a case of beer a client had left next door. I think it had warmed in his car too long.

Our new values were hard to hang on to during a time of such stress. Of an evening, or just any ol' time, really, Jamalee would say such things as "I guess banks are a bad idea these days," or "There *was* a chop shop over past Cabool—they'd probably put us to work," or "I don't imagine you know of any wacky well-to-do folks who keep their mattress stuffed with twenty-dollar bills, do you, Sammy?"

I never answered out loud, merely made faces.

That gun was in the house, on her mind, and at each sunset I could feel we'd edged a bit closer to outright crime.

Already I could hear steel doors clanging and smell a lunch tray of shit-on-a-shingle and taste weak tea.

Then came that evening when the sunset depicted pink fingers raking a general blue and the ad appeared in *The Scroll*: Waitress position at Country Club. Nice atmosphere, $ potential.

West Table, Mo., is a town that exists sure enough—it's all there, the houses and shops and traffic lights, the church spires and shotgun shacks—but it's not a town that stands out special from all the other towns you've drove past without slowing down. The country club perched where the town once ended, though now more new but not special town has popped up to curl around it.

The lane leading in has great tall pine trees edging it, giving off that wonderful shade those trees give and that smell that makes you want to nap and dream. A golf course occupied both sides of the lane. The lane had been paved black and awful smooth.

"I don't know about this," Jamalee said.

Jason leaned up and patted her head.

"Just be yourself and smile."

"Be myself," she said. "Be myself—that's what has got me to here."

Her hair belonged yet in a garden; she'd brushed on a green eye shadow and painted her lips a red one shade lighter red than her hair, the kind that makes lips look wet. Golden hoop earrings dangled. She wore a short, short black dress with bare shoulders and a snug fit. Spike heels elevated her above the category of midget.

The country club building lolled amongst a handsome stand of elder pines. The place had three levels but not in a stack, sort of in a spread, with a separate patio area at each level. The patios had round glass tables with, like, seaside umbrellas over them, striped real bright. The outside walls were of wood and native Ozark stone. The wood had been painted cream.

There were sounds from a swimming pool I couldn't see.

"Oh, man, I don't want to go in there."

I found a space and parked.

"Jam," I said, "we can stay or we can go."

"I can't just go. I *must* go in. I just must."

"So, do what you've got to do, or hush up about it, one."

The girl eased from the car, inhaled mightily, and went toward the door walking strong, stabbing those spike heels with every step. She kept her chin in the air and sent her body after it.

It got near to lunchtime and the parking lot filled. The members drove a lot of lush vehicles, mostly big-assed things a sharecropper could've raised a family in. There were some trucks with extended cabs and bloated wheels and several low-slung sporty chariots.

I had taken a seat on a narrow log rail that bordered the parking lot, beneath the pines in the casket-smelling shade. I avoided eye contact with the members who went by, plenty of them wearing golf cleats so they sounded like slow ponies on a hard road.

Jason had decided to walk inside, see what the delay was, tell Jamalee we're getting hungry, getting hot.

In a short time the two glass doors shove open the way saloon doors at cowboy bars did, and Jamalee stomps out with a pair of men flanking her. She's poking those spike heels down like she's trying to stab through to a vital organ.

She says, her neck tense, "Yeah, well, I'll tell you what *I* think is ridiculous—you assholes are. That's what."

"That's fine," one fella says. Both fellas are dressed in that summertime-casual look that would be mighty dressy down in Venus Holler. "Just leave the club's property, miss."

"Yeah," the other one says, "you're giving the members a sight to have nightmares over."

People coming in and people coming out began to stop. An amused little crowd was acquired. There were diamond rings, gold watches, shoes so ugly they must've cost a pretty penny, and Redneck Riviera tans. These folks were up high in the pay scales and insisted that you know it.

"I already got nightmares," Jam said, "and you assholes are in every one."

"You want me to call the police? I will. I'll call the police. Is that what you want?"

"I want you to kiss my ass and call it orchid."

"Every time you open your mouth, miss, you show why you don't belong here, in the club."

Soon as I got over there, close to Jam, I saw Jason coming through the crowd from behind. The crowd sensed he was with her, I guess, and gave way, until he stood beside his sis.

The other fella who'd brung her out is maybe forty-five, or in that phase of life, and he's had a few drinks, I'd predict, and is standing there like a six-foot piss hard-on. He says, looking at the Merridew kids, "You people are the *lowest* scum in town."

The crowd mutters and titters.

This expression of utter frankness takes over Jason's beautiful face, and he says, "I don't think we're the *lowest* scum in town." He didn't argue that we weren't scum, just disputed our position on the depth chart. It has always hung with me that it was *Jason* who spoke up for us. "Shoot, there's folks—"

"Oh, shut your salad hole, nancy boy." Mr. Piss Hard-on reaches over and pushes a finger into Jason's chest and keeps pushing. "You are an abomination in the eyes of God, and you also get on my fuckin' nerves. Disease-ridden—"

Baby Jam reached the man's face with a swung purse; then her tomato head bent and she bulldozed it at his belly. He didn't care much for that. He got his hands around her throat.

An old elegant gent with whitish hair and a vanilla suit with a blue bow tie, said, "Hey now. Hey now, fellas, hold on here. Hold on!"

Jason hopped to it, bit the fingers of Mr. Piss until he

let loose, then made a slack, floppy fist, not a very useful one, and kind of half threw a punch.

The man smiled like Santa Claus showed up unscheduled and brought him a punching bag that makes rewarding noises.

You could hear people suck for breath, mostly women, I think. One said, softly first, then again and again louder, "You don't have to smack that boy."

Jason tried to stand in there. His efforts were sort of valiant, but pathetic and comical, too, and mostly just a waste of his carbohydrate energy and nerve. The noises he made are probably still being imitated around there. He was handled as easy as a cat handles a guppy that has squirted out of the tank to the shag carpet.

Two members restrained Jamalee.

"You don't have to smack that boy."

There was a mean redness on one of the kid's cheeks, a blood spot below his nose, a look of permanent humiliation.

I guess this is where you uncover what "together" actually adds up to. This is the bunch that would have me. Multiply that by plenty.

I can't say I knew for sure what was called for.

I stepped to the side of the fuss and feathers and hit the man a stomach punch that tore him from his hinges and sat his ass down.

"Now I *am* calling the police."

"Fair fight," I said. I got my face close up to the man still standing. I let him understand that there was oodles of danger in me; my head wobbled loose, three ticks off center. This scary face is all them such as me has to show this other world, the world in charge of our world, that musters any authority, gets any reluctant respect at all. If us lower elements didn't show our teeth plenty and act fast to bite, we'd just be soft, loamy dirt anybody could walk on, anytime, and you know they would, too, since even *with* a show of teeth there's a grass-less path worn clear across our brains and backs. "He asked for it."

I spotted a flicker in the man's eyes, and that's all I spotted before my ribs sprang loose and tried to eat my liver, or that's what it felt like. My vision got suddenly consumed by black. Nose, cheek, chin scraped pavement. My breakfast bounced on me and splattered out. The crowd went "Uhh."

"Fair fight," somebody said, quoting me for ridicule. "He asked for it."

I rolled over and looked up from the blistering pave-ment, and this dude in one of those ugly green uniforms janitors wear stood over me. He wasn't a youngster— maybe fifty. He might've been five foot nine inches tall, but he seemed four feet wide. His hands had those humpy roadhouse knuckles that have been focused on in plenty of X-ray rooms on plenty of Saturday nights. His hair was gray, and the sun had burned him brown as meat loaf. The name over his pencil pocket said *Burt*. His eyes kept on me and he grinned and said, "That's a special haircut you got, son. You mow it that way on purpose?"

If I'd've had that pistol handy, several histories would've took a hard turn at that exact instant. I would've let two rounds off in his fuckin' kneecaps just to hear the bone-crack music. I would've put one in his mother-fuckin' head then and called it a happy accident. It was good, I suppose, that the pistol sat way across town, on a closet shelf, but it surely increased the heap of scorn dumped our way and received.

"Eat shit," I said.

"Okay, son. I'll need to roll you in batter and fry you up, first, prob'ly pour on ketchup."

Oh, ol' Burt was the comedy smash of the summer with the crowd of members, there, in that parking lot. They tee-heed, haw-hawed from down deep, snorted, pulled their sunglasses down and dabbed their giggly eyes.

That's when Jamalee went off, lost it, stood back and let her rant come up and out of her, screaming.

She'd come all the way unleashed.

14

It's Medical Tonight

Sometimes nature has this look where you want to hoot and shout accusations because the look seems so unbelievable, an obvious fake. I study these looks for the brief reward of them, and that night nature tossed me such a look. Rain clouds, all dark and muttering, were mobbing up out west, but long finger bones of sunlight showed through and played the range of colors like a range of musical notes, making a tune of colors from pink to plum and back to yellow all across the rim of the world.

Then the look went down, sank away, and night took control. You could smell the rain marching this way, and hear it, but you couldn't see the clouds. I occupied the Ford alone, as we'd all slunk our separate ways since getting whipped at the country club. I had the King singing to me. My knuckles had scraped down to the ooze, and my ribs kept messing with me, shooting pain like rockets if I moved too sudden.

I sat there trying to avoid certain thoughts—the kind that'll chew the meat clean out of your head if you open their cage. I didn't have any liquor. I wanted to block those certain thoughts. All I'd ate was beans and dessert. I could've stood some liquor, or crank, or maybe snorted some Mexican brown, even.

I didn't know what to do anymore.

Now that I had *values* I was terrible slow in reaching decisions. You get to parsing out right from wrong, and half-right from half-wrong, and sort-of this from sort-of that, on down to both ways suck horrible but this way sucks one horribleness less.

Jesus Christ. It can take you two days to decide on breakfast.

I don't guess I was very long out there in the rumbling night before Bev came over and helped herself to the passenger's seat. She had two bottles of beer, which smelled to me as gold would smell if it smelled.

"Beer man," she sang low. "Cold beer here."

"You are beautiful."

Bev watched me do the deed to the first bottle. Then she held the other out to me. "Go on, Sammy, you take it, I'm *fine*."

I took a deep drink.

"You sure? I mean, it's your beer."

"Slow down, slow down—I'm not going to ask for it back. You'll start belchin'. Take sips for a while. I love this song. It gives me tingles."

The song was "I'm Left, You're Right, She's Gone."

"He ain't called the King for no good reason."

"I admire what you did today. What you tried to do."

"I came up short. It's happened before, but I almost can't stand it."

"Sounds like you don't feel eager for that rough stuff."

"I ain't. I ain't eager. I don't like it at all, but it's always on my menu."

"That makes what you did even better, Sammy. You faced your fear and ate it."

"It's been eatin' back some, but this beer's slowin' it down."

She reached over to my face and fanned her fingers near the pavement scrapes on my cheek and chin and the thin scab along the underside of my nose. They didn't hurt much, really, but still that wind flutter felt nice; merely the attention helped, I'd guess.

"Don't fret," she said, staring at my face. "You weren't that pretty to start with. If you get scars it'll just add *mystery* to you."

Her feet were bare. The toenails were painted pearl. She turned and sat with her back to the door and plopped her feet on my lap. There was an enchanting stripe of smell leaking from her toward me. She wore a pale green dress, with a thin strap around the neck to hold it on, but her shoulders weren't covered and if she leaned forward part of her tits teased you from the side. Hot summertime attire; I've always dug it. Her hair was down and beaming in the dark.

"You don't think I'm pretty?"

"You're pretty tall. You're pretty lean."

"Pretty thirsty."

"Pretty horny—right?"

Well, she didn't have to invite me twice. I gingerly hopped a little sideways and got to her, still holding that beer bottle 'cause there was no flat place to stand it, and started on her neck. I suppose I steered that free hand south a bit too eager to be called smooth.

"Whoa, now, Sammy, take your time, take your time. I don't turn into a pumpkin at midnight or nothing. You've got plenty of time. Kiss me awhile. I'm not about to run, hon. Kiss me on the lips."

I tossed the bottle out the window. Maybe there was a swig left.

"I might not be at my best, Bev, all banged up this way."

"Oh, relax. We're just a couple of blondes, out in the night, willing to have fun. And fun is here. So have it, hon, have it."

Raindrops pinged on the Ford, heavy drops falling straight to strike the hood or the roof and sound like rim shots. The music blended sort of okay. The wind got pushy.

I broke from one clinch for air, and said, "You ain't havin' me be Skeets Benvenuti in your mind, are you?"

"Why, no, huh-uh."

" 'Cause truly, I don't care if you do. If you want."

"No, listen, hon. What I've been needing is a little midnight redneck therapy, and, baby, that's *you*."

I went back in for more, and mumbled, or maybe it was murmured, "Aw, I've been in need of this."

"I know, I know. Sometimes it's the only cure, a medical treatment."

"It's medical tonight, Bev. I'm grateful you're the doctor."

"Let's go in my house, hon, to the bed. I don't want you to bruise your young self when I bounce you off the walls."

She, too, favored candles. Four or five flickered. The rain had turned serious and gusts tossed the white curtains around and made candle flames hop.

"Oh, boy, hon," she said. "I forgot *all* my secrets for a minute there." She sat up a bit and reached for a cigarette, lit it. "I'll bet you'll remember my name now."

Apparently I'd said Marsha one time, at a moment she found funny.

Sex is the thing you can get the furthest behind in but catch up to the fastest. Three and a half months of want had been drained away, and I had two months more of want to tap into after a minute or so.

I said, "Do you think it speaks ill of me that I could be happy here?"

"Not *ill*, but it speaks of you."

I always did like to figure I've done most everything between the sheets twice, but Bev had done most everything between the sheets twice with most *everybody*, and I couldn't claim close to that. I sure couldn't. I've pondered it a lot, but I couldn't lay claim to such battalions of sack memories. Bev could wiggle here and wiggle there and get special feelings running wild in me without opening her eyes. Just a twitch and a lick and a secret touch and I was in way over my head and happy.

"Sammy, after you lay with a woman you don't start thinkin' it amounts to a big deal, do you? You don't start to grab ahold, gum up the works, butt your own opinions in, do you?"

"Not lately."

"Not *lately*?"

"Not ever. Except once."

"Uh-huh. Marsha?"

"Don't say that name."

We made a trip to the kitchen, naked. Bev looked wonderful by candlelight and tasty by the light of the refrigerator. I had a beer, she had wine, we both had a joint. We stood around in there, naked, drinking, smoking, like we'd journeyed to one of those nightclubs I guess they have in Greenwich Village, or Hong Kong, or wherever. She rested my balls in her palm, closed her fingers around them, and looked out the window at rain laying siege to everywhere.

That other two months of want went away: standing there in the kitchen for about two weeks' worth, up against the counter, then on back to bed for the big gush.

Candlelight, cigarette, slow breathing.

"You never say who you are, Sammy. Why is that?"

"You just said who I am."

"But who're your people?"

"You all are."

"No, I mean your blood parents."

"I can't say much good talkin' about them."

"You can't find a good thing to say about your mom, even?"

"She's not around anymore. That's a good thing."

We both dozed. Lightning strikes and thunder rattled

us up from deep good sleep. I stared at the ceiling quite a while; the shadows moved with interesting intentions there.

I thought I heard footsteps, then I *knew* I heard footsteps, and I had a fearful instant wondering whose footsteps those might be and was there a way out of here.

I shook Bev, and when her eyes opened the light was turned on.

"I thought so," Jamalee said. "We need you, Sammy. Get some clothes on."

She and Jason both dripped. They were in regular clothes, soaked. Mud rimmed their shoes.

"I'm kind of—"

"We *need* you. It's important."

Bev said, "You forget how to knock? On doors? I've always asked you to knock."

"You been havin' fun, Bev? Fucked you another Ringo, have you? That makes how many, now, in thousands?"

"Oh, baby Jam—you need to take you a whole day off from whining, sometime, and grow the fuck up during it."

Bev made a move to get out of bed, and Jam and Jason both went "No! No!" Jamalee added, "Bev, we've told you to *never* walk naked in front of us. *Never. Ever.*"

Jamalee's tent dress had been folded around her by rain and tucked in at a couple of places. She held a bottle by the neck that looked to contain rum.

"Jason?" I said.

"Why, yes, sir."

"That wall behind you, there, looks a whole lot like England, understand?"

"Oh, don't you have a high opinion of yourself now."

"Study England so I can get dressed, will you?"

He did face that way, then shook like a dog, spraying a mess of drops.

I pulled on my clothes. I don't know what Jamalee looked at. Nothing that was in that room, I don't imagine. She seemed as though maybe she'd upped her normal pill dose and achieved a highly amped state. .

"There's things wrong," she said. "Things we can set right. Things we can do about wrong things. Wrong things to make right *listen* and say sorry."

Bev shook her head, pulled the sheet to her chin, lay back flat.

"I sense you've got a problem workin' on you," she said. "But ya'll just be sure to let *that* problem stay *outside* of me, hear?"

I got my finger stuck up the pig's ass, you know, to keep him from squealing. He wrestled against me some, and his chest rose and dropped fast, but he stayed there in my arms while I carried him to Rod's truck. My finger felt hot. This finger trick is an old-time farmer's story, it always comes up at nut-cuttin' time, but I'd never actually been in a situation where I needed to stick a finger up there and see if this story held true.

Mostly it held true, though there were grunts and such that sounded close to squeals, yet you couldn't *quite* fairly call them squeals. These pigs hefted at about seventy–eighty pounds, and they'd been penned right near a rock road, somewhere over east of town. We only took three. All three had that black-white-black banding running around their bodies—is that Poland Chinas?

I didn't use the finger on the first pig, and he made too much noise. The other two didn't hardly—I guess that finger poke worked as a sort of surprise pacifier to young pigs.

The rain kept beatin' down. The farmhouse sat proba-bly a hundred yards over. The dogs must've crawled under the porch, because they didn't bark once.

The kids only just stood there in the mud watching me rustle those pigs, their mouths pulled back in silent *yuck!* poses. They hadn't actually interacted with livestock to any useful degree, so, even though this was all Jamalee's idea, *I* did the actual wrangling and toting and finger business.

I heaved the last pig into the truck bed, and he went straight to the burlap bags of ear corn we'd found in the metal feed bin. I bent down to the rainwater pooling in low spots around my boots and churned that pig pacifier extra frantic, to and fro.

"Get in the truck," I said. "Give me that rum." I splashed just a teensy amount on that finger. The alcohol brought back a sanitary feeling. "Let's us get, before we get shot."

The plot was that after this night the country club would never be the same. The golf course part, anyhow. The pigs and their sharp hooves and snuffling snouts and hearty appetites would get out there in the gooey mud and rain and wreak horrors on the delicate golf greens so nothing would roll straight there ever again.

See, the truck couldn't get on the course; posts had been sunk at the cart paths that left enough space for golf carts to pass but not other vehicles. Jamalee knew about those posts, hence the pigs.

So, we herded the three pigs between the posts, towards the nearest green. Water stood on the grass section, the fairway it seems they call it, a couple of inches deep, and that rainstorm still showed energy. All our head hairs lay plastered to skulls. Clothes had got sogged and made you feel fat and captured by something thick.

The pigs liked the weather. They followed the ear corn.

Jason carried a bag of corn, as did Jamalee, and they held ears out so those pigs would follow, corn being a language the pigs understood. Their pointy hooves gouged everywhere they stepped.

I'd had me an idea and lugged a strand from Rod's rusty logging chain. It was a big sincere chain, no toy, weighted to do heavy chores. I drug it along and kept sampling the rum.

I held the bottle to Jam, who said, "No thanks, Sammy, that's for you. Rum might *clash* with my pharmaceuticals."

I had only been lookin' to get a buzz on, but of a sudden I was boom-boom-boom drunk.

At the first green the kids tossed down a dozen ears of corn and the pigs started stamping about, shoving each other aside, sliding in the wet, turning the grass up and pushing it away in long swaths like scraping thumbnails through the icing on a cake. The pigs made a considerable mess of that green, but Jam and Jason and me hadn't let go, hadn't begun enjoying ourselves yet. It was like a party that wouldn't quite start happening.

We herded those pigs with boot toes and shouts and whistles, from one green to the next.

At about the third green I stretched the logging chain across the heart section, then stomped the links into the mud.

"Get on," I said. "Jamalee, stand on that chain."

When she did, me and Jason pulled. The pigs grunted and ran around, still enchanted by those ears of corn. We pulled the chain between them, scattering them some, and Jamalee stood back there, arms spread, skiing on the heavy chain.

"Putt this, assholes!"

That chain ripped serious damage into the putting surface. You could've laid pipe in the trenches we ripped there.

Jam had to ski each green after that. Me and Jason laughed crazy and the party was on. She glided back there, her hands held up to the rain, and shouted the shouts she'd shouted in the parking lot all over again. Those shouts had connected her and Jason more than slightly to those rich house break-ins. She'd screamed some pretty catty shit about who kept what where, and who had a mansion but drank jug wine, and who had undies that she and Jason found to be perfect fits, and what beds they'd peed on.

Her comments had shook me more than those humpy-knuckled fists had.

Anyhow, us and the pigs did a fine wicked job on the fat cats' playground. The greens went bald that night, and we three screamed insults to the heavens and rejoiced in the storm.

Something that needed saying was getting said this night.

Jason cut loose, danced around on the mud, kicked up his heels, and danced with glee, his beautiful face turned to meet the rain.

The way he looked then has stayed with me.

15

As Far as Time Goes

There was no call to ask each other who they were, because you could just look at them and understand right now that they were a news flash you'd been hoping to not be a party to. The aerial on their car kept whipping in long loose silvery whips even after they'd parked and started walking up the dirt drive. The both of them had ties on, the skinny shoelace sort, but not jackets. Their walking pace threw mud. Pistols made their belts sag, but their chins were raised.

The three of us stood there in a silent short line behind Bev's screen door, facing out. This bunch of kids were laughing loud across the road, busting things in the ditch there, and fireflies were coming on. That antenna still was whipping silvery and wobbling atop their white sedan. Biscuit loped over as they came closer and got behind them. He snorted air and his tail made friendly motions.

Both of them kept their expressions squashed flat and nodded toward us behind the screen.

The one with a gray beard said, "Do all of you want to come?"

Concerns had set in a lick after supper the evening before. Jason didn't show. Bev brung home ribs from Otto and Belle's, plus slaw and beans, which they say he loved and were in the absolute classic range and flavor of barbecue, but the boy never did show to eat. He'd been told about the upcoming ribs at noon, too. The concerns made only a faint beep in Jamalee's head just then. She paced off and looked out the windows a bunch of times. These ribs were dry-rubbed in the downriver fashion and cooked slow, slow, slow, and even the beans had caught a smoky taste, so up until the leftovers from his plate joined their kindred in my tummy I didn't exactly percolate too wild about where, oh, where, young Jason could be.

Bev and me both said over and over about ten times that he was seventeen years old and probably making a friend off away from here somewhere.

"You don't really know him," Jamalee said. "He's a very precise person as far as time goes, and also he's a person who loves Otto and Belle's ribs and he'd call if he got this late and say save him some."

It wasn't that far where they carried us to in their car. The radio kept making noises, electric malfunction sounds, and sometimes voices came across the air but I never did catch a complete thought that was said. I sat over on the side of the backseat, Bev rode in the middle. The cops never turned around or said a thing. They drove us on across the creek which has a name I don't know on that narrow black bridge with the sign that warns you suddenly the bridge is one-lane only. The road was paved to just beyond there then switched to rock and started to climb.

I could hear Jamalee breathing; her breaths were sucked in slow and off the beat, like she had to keep remembering to inhale.

Up the hill shy of the crest there was a sharp turn onto a rut road. The turn had gotten a mud bank built up by spinning tires and we went high to make the turn, then shot down and bounced on in a pretty rough way for a while. The bounces made you wince, and us in the back were bashed into each other a few times. Nobody spoke anything.

I could see the water when we stopped. There was a rough log cabin across the pond and the water was green and the pond long and narrow. Two or three vehicles were parked ahead and an ambulance was one of them. This was now twilight, and a variety of men stood around the water's edge shining flashlights.

Once we got out and had those silvery whips above us, the young cop held out a little blue jar full of that mentholated chest rub you use when your chest rattles in winter. He opened it and smeared a big glob right where a mustache would go if he had one, then pushed the jar at Bev.

"Huh?" she went.

"It's been mighty hot, ma'am. The water, even, is warm this time of year. This cuts the—I'm sorry—this stuff here cuts the smell you're goin' to find."

When Tomato Red would get to chattering and speculating hot and fevered she couldn't hardly be interrupted. She could sure talk a gang of doom when she got going that way: The evil fates were biding their time in the attic of that empty house down the road just watching for a chance, and serious misery kept hovering just north of your brain pan holdin' a pool cue—that sort of stuff. Not those words, but those were the messages.

Such speech had spurred me out and about town the next noon after those ribs with her looking for any sign of Jason. The Ford needed oil and a tune-up. This Pinto pooted small gray distress signals from the tailpipe and sounded like a chain-smoker at a cold dawn and practically shrieked for a civil rights lawyer when I forced it up hills.

Jamalee dangled her tomato from the other window, not too eager to be seen in my shit car but scanning up and around the roadside, checking faces and alleys.

You'd have to even now say that the day shaped up beautiful: big blue above and runny-butter hot with a sporty breeze shooing tender smells on by. Everybody came out of his house. Bicycles and baby carriages and shoppers rolled around the square. Even the drunks at the Tiny Spot Tavern between the square and the stockyards had wobbled into the light out front and took sunbaths with beer cans in hand.

At Romella's we got told it had been a normal day. The day before. Jason had come and gone as was his custom, and said or did not a thing odder than usual.

In the car again, I asked, "Could he have a secret life?"

"Huh-uh. Not him. He just barely had an *un*-secret life."

They hit him with points of light from a fistful of angles and one held steady on his chest and the others slid away from him, peeked back at some segment of his dead self, then slid off and away again. He was a lump laid at the water's edge. He still wore everything, including his shoes. The pond kept making noises, spit-up noises, like a baby that don't care for mashed carrots. Let's say it was the wind. They had him there flat on his back but his arms held out still sideways above the ground. There were fish-hooks in him. Fishhooks trailing leader lines, stuck in him up here and down there, one in the cheek of his face, two in the purple hand I could see. The pond sounded ready to puke.

Someone official asked, "That's him, ain't it?"

Jamalee leaned forward and just looked and looked stricken, man, her face froze like a statue that got made at a moment of deep, deep, soundless fear.

"That's my son," Bev said. She sagged at the knees, then pushed herself up straight. "I remember those socks."

Lake's Market stood there like the gateway to Venus Holler. You couldn't come in or get out without going past the place. The building was old, wooden and splashed white with paint, with a pocked concrete walkway across the front raised maybe four feet from the parking spots. There were only three parking spots, and even from the coop you could hear horns honking at each other and gruff voices now and again saying *come on, buddy, move your ass* type of comments.

I had lucked into a spot and we both went inside. I always did enjoy Lake's: There were no hard-and-fast rules about where things would be on the shelves, they sold every different kind of cheap beer you could think of, cheap beers from all over that he would sell by the can, and he kept a humongous old yellow cat that weighed about twenty pounds and could cut farts that ran every-body out of there hooting.

"Well, hello there, Jamalee."

"Mr. Lake, how are you?"

"No complaints." He was a tall narrow stoop-shouldered black-wavy-haired man. "Hey, Sammy."

I nodded but she spoke. "Have you seen my brother?"

"No," he said, and sort of laughed. "Can't say I have." He sort of laughed when he said most everything. I don't know what causes that, but he was that way. Hotter'n hades, you might say, and he'd laugh. My wife split to Nashville with the ice-cream-truck driver; or, I drew the short straw at Happy Bark and won't be employed any-more; My mom married a cop—he'd laugh at all those things and two million more. "I ain't seen him for, oh, I don't know. He almost always pokes his head in when he goes by."

"I know he does," she said.

"He's a nice young fella."

"Uh-huh."

"He's gone, is he? Since how long?"

"One night."

A long bolt of laughter unrolled from him.

"Why, Jamalee," he said, "I expect that boy has been holed up somewhere learning the *secrets of the night*. He's an awful handsome—"

"Nope," she said, and we left.

I waved to him, to show courtesy, as the door slapped behind us.

She sat over there in the Ford, her face expressing several things not good. The possible answers had got loose in her head and the bad ones chewed her deep.

I flip-flopped my own emotions and smiled.

"He probably just didn't run," I said. "Lake's likely on the money. He's up . . ."

"*No, no, no!*"

Aw, this foolishness had no bottom to it, and we had begun to realize that.

Whoever set it up set it up to look like nature done it. Jason's nature and the big nature both—his to get him in that pond foolishly, the big one to make waste of a fool.

I didn't study him much, him there on the mud bloating and colored different from his settling blood. There were cans of drunk pop-top cocktails tossed about near where he laid. Whiskey sours and Cuba libres and margaritas.

The law didn't seem to be interested in the cans, or the fishhooks, or the body either.

"I'd say he dove in here, probably been drinkin' and got all sweaty, and swam out to where he was snagged on these ol' hooks and lines," one of them said. "There's a rough bottom to this pond, prob'ly a thousand hooks broke off out there."

"Pretty new hooks," I said.

"I guess some could be."

William the John Law had been in the crowd there, and he stepped forward and sort of took over. He said, "I sure am sorry, Bev. This is a sad, sad thing. I guess the boy didn't swim so great, did he?"

"He wasn't much for swimmin', no."

"I see that."

"I mean," she said, "Jason didn't swim *at all*."

The officials looked away from her, shined their lights toward the pond, scanned the beams over the dark water.

"Ah, well," William said, "then I guess it's no wonder he drowned, is it?"

16

Belong to a Reason

Only one plank of ham was left but I dropped it into the black skillet and fried it up. It was one of those sort of particle-board hams made by taking different pieces of ham and mashing them together. To me it tasted fine and went great with this potato dish some girl from his high school class mixed up and dropped by. Romella herself brought the ham, and I'd been eatin' from it since four days back. The whole holler seemed to slump more. The food had been laid out over in Bev's place. I was the only one you could say tried to eat much, stay strong. Everything had got to feeling gray. There'd been a couple of pies, rhubarb and peach, and a plastic vat of a salad mixture in a thin dressing. None of them wanted to come inside but they did want to show their faces and leave those sympathy dishes for the family. *The Scroll* told of his passing a short drop down the page from another article on the future of the battered golf course. The funeral attracted a small circle and featured no sermon and went by in a blink. Things flurried in my head. A couple of jack-leg ministers fell by but gave up pretty quick. The girls from the salon donated plenty of other foods to snack on. Tim Lake of an evening sent a bucket of crispy chicken. Trains roared past and it seemed yelled spiteful I-told-you-so's sent from across the nation. The days felt sad and slow, and him dying was treated like a thing that deserved a reward because we'd been eating fat and richly since that boy choked under for the third time in that scummy green pond.

Mother and daughter took to grieving in their separate houses which I wandered back and forth between. Some fellas who'd done Bev left a bottle of scotch and several kinds of wine with handsome labels. Neither of the gals hardly ate much at all. They huddled and hunkered differently. The scotch suited me. Death and liquor seem to always call for each other. Call and response. I had let myself leak for the first time since that other time. Throw your emotions loose. The dog moaned and scratched and begged for petting. My head showed four movies at once and around the clock. Tears dropped like walnuts.

At the one house, I happened on Jamalee all curled in a baby ball, her droopy blinky eyes ringed with tired from loss and pills, and she looked at me and said, "I'm trying to escape. Escape to anywhere, but I'm not. I'm not going anywhere. There isn't any anywhere, is there? Another hoax on me."

And later she again spoke from the baby ball. "Hey, Sammy, I'm floating. There's a smart breeze flying me— show your ticket, grab hold."

At the other house, Bev would smile out of some reflex. Her face didn't mean what her brief smile said. She didn't drink much, really, except for wine. Cigarettes calmed her, or some such, and her shack filled with smoke and she sat there staring through the smoke straight at a wall. She avoided windows, kept her eyes fixed on that wall. She sat that way for hour after hour, then another, sipping wine and lighting cigarettes but not saying a word.

Then, when I'd about forgot she sat there, suddenly she says a single line: "There's all kinds of mean business on two legs out there."

The weather didn't help. The weather kept picking at us—nothing but heavy wet heat, sweat, heat, sweat, bugs, bugs, and bad whipped moods. The weather stayed in that attitude of weather where you can't help but wonder just who it is you've pissed off so.

But I had been wondering that anyway.

Light was sliding into dark and Bev talked again: "Oh, did I just say anything?"

"Naw."

"I didn't just now blurt something?"

"I didn't hear it."

"Whew! Thank God."

I went away then and ate that last fried plank of ham and thought and thought and paced. The scotch got to asking questions.

I think one of our cardinal fuckups is how we insist that even vicious whimsical crazy shit needs to make sense, add up, belong to a reason. We lay this pain on ourselves—there must be a reason behind this horror, there must, but I ain't adequate to findin' it, and that's my fault, so torture me some more.

Way past nightfall I flicked the TV on and sat in the squeaky rocker. Some show played, kids who drive Porsches to high school and eat in sit-down restaurants on their own, but there's this emptiness in them, apparently, bigger than the beach. They were folks you'd like to meet sometime and leave in a car trunk at the airport. The show, though, was candy to the eyes. I rocked and watched.

Bev kept on just sitting there staring at that empty wall like it was a mirror.

When Jamalee came over she smacked the door shut

and Bev and me turned to see her. She'd been mighty roughed up by her feelings for a few days and looked it. Her hair had gotten slack from being dirty and those tiny hands quaked a bit and her face had been screwed down tight. She put everything important into one stinky sentence and flung it in the middle of us: *"He'd never go swimming!"*

17

Him Needs

It could've been a happy dreamy spot on a hot summer
night. A place for a few cool beers and maybe a bout of
taboo courtship with somebody who sniffed and claimed
not to know you in daylight. It could've been the secret
spot you snuck away to with your secret eighth-grade girl-
friend from the big brick house on the hill and skinny-
dipped and made her pregnant in the moonlight and
ruined everything for yourself in that town even worse
and not exactly brightened her days much either, except it
was the spot where Jason died and you couldn't quite feature the other stuff happening there anymore.

The lights from the Pinto busted the dark over the
pond and let us see the green water and green scum glow.

"That water looks icky," Bev said.

"It's just water that don't move," I said. "Scum'll flat skim over still water."

"Your point is?"

"In heat like this you might swim in it anyhow."

"Not with all those hooks."

"I don't believe in those hooks. There ain't any pond anywhere with hooks and lines in it *that* thick."

Jamalee said, "Prove it to us, huh? Prove your point, Sammy."

She stood there tiny and looked even more tiny in the shirt she wore. The shirt was white and long-sleeved, one of Jason's, and it draped on her loose with the tails hanging down her body to where a short skirt would finish. The sleeves were rolled back to her elbows and she wore peach-colored track shorts and blue rubber sandals, the kind for in the shower. Her voice had taken on a crackly croaky quality from being so forlorn and leeched of pep, I guess.

"I wouldn't be scared to," I said.

"Of course you wouldn't."

"It can't be that bad."

"No, no, huh-uh. So dive in."

"The water probably feels good."

"The *water* probably does."

"I don't believe in those hooks."

"Prove it, baby, with a real big splash."

I walked to the edge of the green water. I looked out over the pond and it wasn't too much. It wasn't too much to swim across or anything. I picked my way along the bank and at each step the nearest and next frog would leap to the pond. There were scads of them there. You couldn't see them, but as I walked they plopped the water in a rippling rhythm like piano keys being swiped from one end to the other and swiped at whatever pace I walked at. The moon wasn't lit up very bright. A grab bag of dank smells were smeared around and about that pond.

"Sammy?" Bev did a sort of shouting whisper. "Sammy, hon, where are you?"

Her voice brought me back to the light. The headlight shafts were hectic from bugs flying dizzy close to the car but they thinned out as the light pushed away over the pond. Jamalee stood there on the downslope, slipping her sandals over long grass blades, looking down; then she spun in a mindless tight circle and sighed.

I undressed fast, over to one side of the headlight beams, pulled everything off until I became dressed only in boxer-type skivvies which I kept wearing. There were little sharpnesses underfoot straightaway. Gravel, I guess, and shards from shattered bottles that had gotten shattered by folks who'd been on this spot being dreamy years ago and busted their bottles and left the shards as a signature instead of initials on a tree trunk inside a heart.

Bev saw me disrobed and said, "You don't have to. You don't have to get in that icky pond, hon, if you'd rather not."

"I've been in worse."

"You swim strong, I hope."

"Strong enough for floods."

The scum parted some where I hit that water, parted like a bullet hole, then began to heal back around me. The temperature felt close to body heat, but I don't guess it was. But it felt like it was and that temperature acted as a relaxant, better than a pill, and my muscles began to ease lengthwise and come unknotted. My feet touched bottom; the scum rose to my nipples.

Things had fallen into that pond since it began, I would imagine, back when. Things had fallen in or washed in or got tossed in and sank to the mud bottom and acquired that slippery coating of green stuff that looked like cheap felt when you saw it but made your feet slide from things with a quick jolt plenty of times. You could find a place to stand, but walking in that pond was hard. A big assortment of logs especially were underfoot. The logs made a jumble there, riprap such as bass really like to live in. You couldn't walk across that, your feet were always sliding and plunging between logs in the jumble, barking your shins and bruising your ankles.

I tried to keep the light over my shoulder.

There were pairs of eyes all over ahead of me, shining and staying still. You always have to remind yourself that those eyes attach to mere bullfrogs and hope you ain't conning yourself. Those eyes just sit there until you hear the croak and then they're gone and the pond scum swishes a bit.

Bev said, "So? How's the water, Tarzan?"

"Like takin' a bath."

"Uh-huh. Only you don't get clean."

"Right."

"You think I should swim in there?"

"Sure. It's not that bad. It's water. It's water in summer."

Jam said, "I can't swim, and I don't care to."

"But we do," Bev said. "I'll have to trust your opinion, Sammy. Trust that water'll be okay for delicate ol' me."

I could only sort of see her on the bank, behind the light beams, but I could tell she was shedding attire.

"I wouldn't steer you wrong."

"If you say so, hon." Her voice went singsongy and way Southern as she said, "I always have *trusted* in the *kindness* of alcoholic rednecks."

She stepped slowly down the slope to the pond. She put a toe in the water and made a silly shiver like an actress might, pretending the water was cold. Her T-shirt was on yet, a pale blue one, and she had those purple panties on that display just a skinny strap up the crack and look so wonderful. She didn't ease into the pond, but reared back and flew herself out flat in the air and hit the scum like a swan, gliding away from shore with as much grace as the pond would allow. Her hair caught the headlight beams and held them there and shined, it seemed, like a planet.

She swam to me, then we swam together. We set out for the other shore, the grass bank, the far end of the pool beyond where the light ended. Fairly often I'd slow and set my feet down and nowhere did the scum push over my head.

We splashed close together.

Bev said, "This is strange. This is so strange."

"Uh-huh. But I've got this opinion really firm now that you'd have to have help to drown here, Bev. This water ain't much."

"This pond, I don't know, it's making me moody. The strangeness of this. It runs moods over me."

"I ain't felt a single hook."

"No, that's not anything I've felt here either, hon."

The pond heaved around us like a breathing thing that had swallowed us inside its foamy green skin and bad smell. In and out the water went as with a fat thing's quick small breaths after gorging.

"I don't want to believe this," she said. "It's really goin' to hurt if I do."

I saw Jamalee up by the headlights, flitting along the

high lip of the dirt bank that ran around the pond. She continued on the move whenever I glanced that way, that white shirt causing a blur over there that kept bouncing slow sideways above the water.

"You know it's true, Bev. We knew that a li'l bit before and we know it more now. But if we go on and say 'yes, let's believe it' out loud, it'll be mighty hard to sit still anymore. Mighty damned hard."

After then we stroked through the green scum, paddling across the light to where the car parked. We got out there where his body had laid and went on up with water guttering down our butts. I shoved the headlights to dark, and we sat on the Pinto to dry some on the heated hood.

The white blur approached.

"And all your splashing tells you exactly what?" she asked. "Huh? Any answers?"

Twigs and leaves or some type of green matter in clumps and strands and flecks were stuck to Bev and me and we both picked and scraped, making the Ford wiggle as we sat on that warm hood leaking pond water.

"I never touched a hook," I said.

"Me neither."

"I never even *sensed* a hook, you know, or line."

"Ah," Jamalee went. "Ah, yes."

Jamalee stared toward the dark pond and of course

her heart and mind would be making connections between this spot, this spot at night, and some miserable way of death being inflicted on the prettiest boy in the Ozarks.

Pretty didn't help much against mean, and mean had its way right exactly here.

She kept standing there, a nearby blur, her back to the car.

Bev shook loose a couple of straight smokes and I took one to burn the pond-scum taste from my mouth. We puffed a little cloud over our heads. She put her hand on my knee a few times. Her hair had got flattened around her face. There were lots of bug and frog sounds in the dark. I could've drunk a beer.

There was, I guess, too much to say, or think about saying, for us to say much of anything yet.

We hung around that pond until my skivvies dried, dried only to damp, then rolled downhill and returned to the holler, not talking at all—from fear, I think, of what we might have to say.

Later, past midnight, I imagine, I was in Rod's house with Jamalee. A porch light across the street hung there up high and burned like a warning to small craft at sea. Sharp shadows had the walls covered. Jamalee lay inside her nook with the blanket curtain closed and I sat on the cable-spool coffee table hard by the window. Biscuit flopped directly behind me and snored.

There were gangs of angers inside that house. Angers plus fears plus hurt. If this house lived as a human you'd send it to a rest home in the faraway world to receive a cure.

I wasn't going to care much for being lonely again, if that's what was coming. Something was coming. Hunting a new bunch that would have me, I never do enjoy that process. That hadn't been said—get out—it hadn't come to that yet, but I could see that same calamity that always hounded me hunkered at the edge of the campfire light, yawning and picking its teeth, lurking.

In my heart, you see, I knew I could live here.

I didn't want to leave, or be left, either.

Jamalee lay back there behind the blanket curtain, and for extended yawns of time she didn't speak, but when she did it was consistently on the topic of flight, flight to more civilized area codes and the various made-up shit she insisted would be true ways of life in those other classes of world.

"The problem is," she said, "I've never really been any-where. We drove through St. Louis one time at night, I don't remember why, but didn't stop. Then I ran away for adventure when I was fourteen, like anybody would, and found myself in Oklahoma, this little red dirt village not far from Tulsa, which I looked around and thought, This is not the direction to run toward 'cause nothing has changed hardly from home. You might as well be in West Table as Oklahoma, so I came straight back all disappointed."

"There'd be little differences," I said. "There's always little details you don't know about places."

"I'm not fleeing toward 'little details,' Sammy. I want the whole picture painted over and a bunch of squatty shiny fellas in tuxedos making music just out of sight behind the palm trees."

"That place ain't on the map."

"Something close enough to it is."

"You've got a lot of disappointments out there, waitin' to greet you, Jamalee. You talk this mighty tall baloney, but you're smarter'n that, ain't you?"

"I *want* what I *want*."

"You want the future to be impossible, so you're fucked over and short-changed *again*."

"My, my. You learn that deep psycho-stuff in a prison chat group, or Harvard College, or where?"

She was, I know, operating on popped pills, talking at me from way inside a dope mist and her own scared and sort of biggety-acting personality. I could've gone for her heavy, man, if she had ever even gave me a light-headed hint I should. She just wanted me as like a third-string brother, I suspect, and nothing more, and I was willing to take that, too.

"It's common knowledge," I said. "It's found written on most shithouse walls."

I turned about and used my foot to jiggle Biscuit up and alert, end those snores. He stood and shook and made a noise from deep in his chest. He went to sniffing at me.

"C'mon, buddy," I said. We both got to moving slow on our way out. "Ol' Biscuit needs him a walk, don't him?"

Just when we about reached the screen door she said, "Oh, Sammy's the one needs to visit ol' Bev. *Him* needs to get wrecked next door, but him needs to be sure and wear a condom; and also him needs to say, 'Hi, Mom,' for me, would him?"

18

Soap and Pudding

A mess of cats whirled around and about in the dark, visible practically underfoot one second, then *pfft!* and they were gone away altogether like those ideas maybe you'd been told and told about but just didn't get. There was a freight on the way, scolding traffic with its huge horn at each road crossing, a scolding you could hear for miles, this train still four or five roads distant. Two or three citizens were jaw-jackin' the night away at one of the dark houses across the road, which one exactly I couldn't say. Their talk was at that level of loud the too-drunk-to-notice favor. Biscuit broke away in the yard to my Ford and hoisted a rear leg and peed on my front left tire.

He acted younger once he was done. One of the drunks over there had got to explaining some experience he'd gone through that had his congregation snorting and spanking their boots down on the porch steps, most likely pissing the host over there's wife off pretty good.

I'd always craved to be a hero to somebody, which I know sounds fairly lame, but it had truly been in my wishes.

The train had screamed closer and louder and made you comprehend why people throw rocks at them. They really tested your patience and such the way a loud-mouthed motorcyclist in a holding cell might, or a father-in-law so often does on holidays. The train went by huffing like an avalanche late for a date with a flood some-place down the line.

Me and Biscuit went on inside of Bev's shack. I eased the screen door closed so it wouldn't slap. The front room smelled like a bus station. There were stinks in those walls of an age where your great-granddaddy might have left them there, and then that steady application of current sad-assed stinks from cigarettes and liquor and home life layered over and combined with the older gloomy odors to create the complicated stink of right now, this minute.

There was a lamp on over by Bev's green chair, which she was in, slumped. Her head jerked about and her eye-lids flapped as she fought against passing out. A cigarette burned between her fingers and the smoke flew straight up in a thin line.

I guess she heard us.

She raised her face for a look and said, "Oh. I don't feel . . . I don't feel up to wrestlin' you tonight, hon. TV."

"Right," I said. "Rain check."

I stubbed her cigarette in the ashtray. Her eyes eased shut and her chin hit her chest. Biscuit sniffed at her feet, then fell over and stretched flat. I got hold of her shoulder and tugged and she came along as I pulled, following my lead but not quite aware of it, I don't imagine. She just followed to wherever I tugged her and I got her to her bed and into it. She only wore a thin naughty-nightie type thing, so I didn't need to strip her. I tossed the white sheet across her legs and up to her middle.

She didn't look her best.

I went into the kitchen where the beverages were stashed. There was no beer. I looked all up and down inside the fridge. There was no whiskey, either, none that I could find. There was wine, which I consider only for emergencies, and only wine, so I found a plastic blue juice cup and filled it high.

I switched off all the lights in the front room. I lit a menthol from her pack and went to the screen door and stood there looking out, choking on the cigarette and the wine, which was of the Chablis category.

This holler, at night or during the day, either one, had the shape of a collapsed big thing, something that had been running and running until it ran out of gas and flopped down exhausted exactly here. The houses were flung out along this deep crease in the hills and the crease surely did resemble the posture of a forlorn collapsed creature. Scrub timber and trash piles and vintage appliances spread down the slopes and all around the leaning houses to serve as a border between here and everything that wasn't here.

If I knew what to do I'd be willing to do it.

It took three smokes to help me get that wine down. I went into the bedroom then. I'd left a lamp burning in there so there was a tiny bit of light. I skinned myself naked and got into bed, pulled the sheet up.

There were several pictures of Bev hung on the walls of the bedroom that had been taken back when. I could lay there and see them. Back when was her golden age, that was clear. She'd been something for a spell there. I guess the pictures didn't make her sad. Her face and figure used to be the kind you could've used to sell things with: Use this soap, get this face; eat this pudding, get this figure. That sort of thing.

You sure would've sold a lot of that soap and pudding, too.

I laid there with my eyes closed but still saw those

pictures of her in my head, only now they had acquired motion. She was dancing with that old figure, that old face, or laughing and leaning against a Mustang convertible in the sunshine, or, best of all, just walking away from me down a brick walkway in summertime attire but looking back over her shoulder with a daring sort of pouty-lipped look.

Those pictures played on for me in my head, and I experienced a wisp of sadness and a bucket of appreciation. I hadn't quite gotten slowed down to sleep when in came Jamalee walking like the undead, her arms slack at her sides. She didn't say a thing. She had on one of those tents she wore, yellow-colored, and came along with her eyes held almost closed. Her tomato-red head wobbled a bit loose on her shoulders. She got to the foot of the bed, then got on her knees and dog-walked up to the pillows. She was on top of the sheet and she laid down on her back between Bev and me, the sheet like a hammock, sort of, beneath her, and closed her eyes.

"Lights," she said.

I came awake the way a bottle washes to shore. Soft, small nudges bobbed me in that direction and patted me toward eye-opening time, and when I did arrive at that time my eyes rolled open and so did Tomato Red's. There was this jolt of social fright because we had gotten snuggled together while adrift, her tomato beneath my chin, and suddenly came awake and realized it.

The color red filled my vision and the smell of her hair and breath and neck had my nose twitching. I'm fairly certain I had worn a smile in my sleep. My arms had gotten under and around her and pulled her in close and held her there while my body formed around her like a big spoon on a little spoon.

There was a sense of comfort overall.

For maybe one instant I thought she might loll in my arms a spell even while awake, but uh-uh, baby. She began to buck against my hug. She got her fingers into my arms and pulled.

I went ahead and released her.

She spun over to where Bev had slept.

She laid on her side there and our eyes met and I couldn't read her expression too well but I knew she hadn't hated my hug all that bad, either. Not as bad as she acted. She'd wiggled backwards into me a few times, and that ain't much of a brush-off, is it?

Voices were reaching us from another room, which is likely the thing that sparked an end to sleep. The voices were sort of loud and clashing with each other.

Jam listened, then whispered, "That's that cop."

I can't say for certain how Bev got him to come over,

but he was there, William the John Law, in the front room, and they were going round and round with words.

Probably from the sounds of it they stood near the screen door or maybe just inside. He said something about how people pretty often insist something bigger happened than had happened. The smallness of the truth can rub the mind wrong.

She said, "There's absolutely no way, not a chance, that Jason went hiking up to that pond and dove in there when he couldn't swim across a bathtub and also had on his fancy pointy-toed shoes. Huh-uh, huh-uh."

"Aw, Bev, do you know how average that sounds? Shit. I'm always running up on parents who swear their kids would never ever in a million years do what I caught them red-handed doing. I hear this stuff awful regular, Bev."

"Those hooks, that's impossible."

"Bev, the coroner signed off on the drowning."

"He's a *tow-truck* driver, William! Abbott Dell can only maybe, and this is *just* maybe, tell a knife slash from a heart attack."

"He's the elected coroner. He can voucher out for a state boy to do a autopsy."

"But he didn't."

"Each one costs the county so many dollars, Bev, I forgot how much but it's plenty, and they can't do one on every kid who gets drunk and drowns."

The screen door whined, which meant it opened, and the voices went into the yard and were lost to me. I shook out a cigarette from a half-wadded pack on the night table there. The cigarette had a crook in it but burned fine.

I sat on the bed and looked at those photos hung on the wall. Jamalee sat on the bed and looked the other way. The day was going to be another one that made tar bubble and flowers wilt and foul moods general. The smoke hung in the air, no breeze to break it up.

The door whined open again, and whacked shut, and the footsteps shuffled across the carpet and came directly to the bedroom doorway. Bev had on a white dress and no shoes and a real startled facial expression.

"Well, well," she said. "You-all, you didn't tell me something, did you? William said a strange thing. He said, 'What I could investigate and *solve* would be which trashy bunch ruined the golf course. I could *do* that, Bev, and probably today.' " Bev switched her eyes from Jamalee to me to her own feet, then around the circuit again. "I think there might be something major you all need to let me in on, is that not right?"

19

Rock Pavilions

"Just give it to me one leg at a time," Bev had said, and we did that. But Bev wasn't swallowing the whole truth too well. She had a number of objections to it, which she shouted. More or less shouted. Sitting on a green picnic table in the town park with so many other folks about her voice seemed shouted anyhow. Eventually she added, "You crazy babies. You crazy fuckin' babies."

Regular citizens from all the ages were all over the park. They were apparently celebrating some fun moment from history that I don't know about. The picnic tables were coated by plates and sacks and big plastic bowls.

There were grilling burgers and ice chests and lots of watermelons in evidence. I couldn't imagine what big event was being honored this way. Watermelon rinds were scattered by the rusty trash barrels, looking like so many dead green grins. There were quite a few radios playing, mostly carrying the Cardinals game from St. Louis, and kids running loose and toys flung in the air, or batted or kicked there, flying from one big spread of food to some other feast across the way.

Biscuit got frisky from the many fetching smells and the active children. He was a shaggy fur ball of appetite. His nose kept busy trying to inhale the whole range of treat smells that rode on the air.

"What do you mean *skied*?"

I let Jamalee do the explaining, but once in a while I'd put in with a "That's right" or "Yeah, yeah, that's the way it happened."

Biscuit wandered over to the chain fence that went around the swimming pool, which was defunct. The water in the pool was shallow and brown, with paper cups and leaves floating. The mutt sniffed and scouted most of the fence line, then heard something he liked, I think, and jogged over the grass to a man in a white T-shirt and plaid shorts and a three-day beard. The man slipped him a bite of something that he accepted with one big chomp and a tail wag.

"I guess you *could've* found folks worse to mess with, but you couldn't do it around here." Bev got a smoke lit. Her expression, funny enough, didn't express fright or disgust or anything except, I think, anticipation. "If King Kong lived in town I reckon you could've fucked with *him* and been in worse trouble. Or if Frankenstein came from Grace Avenue you could've thrown mud balls at his momma and got a *monster* chasin' after your dumb asses."

"I couldn't let them do me that way. You weren't there to see it, Bev. I couldn't have the regard for me I need to have if I let them do me that way."

"Oh, so what if you were mistreated, baby Jam? So what? You weren't invited. You weren't wanted there. They didn't send for you. Hon, that's the entire purpose of private places—to keep *us* out. You *do* understand that, I *know* you do."

Jamalee sat there and in response shifted into that simmering, sullen posture she could accomplish that left no need for a response via words. She had on shorts in daylight for, I think, the first time I'd ever seen. Shorts and a buttoned-down long-sleeve blue shirt, despite which she didn't seem to be sweating.

I said, "There's times you need to stand tall, you know, show some spirit."

"You call trashing the golf course 'standing tall,' do you?"

169

"A person has to show some spirit—fate just about never shines kindly on chickenshits."

Nearby the table we sat on there stood two rock pavilions that had gotten built by all those hungry hobos and whatnot the government harnessed and put to work back in the Dust Bowl–type days, when starvation was easy to come by and no rain wrung from the sky till too late. The pavilions had roofs and cement floors and held six or eight tables and each had big old brick cooking pits built in against the eastern wall. The pavilions were packed by people. Families, no doubt. They were grilling those wieners that grow plump over heat, that kids seem especially to favor. They had banners hanging that still didn't make it plain to me exactly what great moment from the heydays was getting so celebrated by the general population. The men stood around holding scary long forks and had bellies drooping above their legs, most of them. These old boys thumped their fat bellies proudly, with a kind of strange confidence, like all that fat was so much fat in the bank, fat they figured to retire on someday and live off.

They seemed to like their children.

I saw Biscuit snorting the ground over near there, on a treasure hunt.

"Oh, lordy, do you really believe that crap, hon? You-all think maybe you got you something special going with the spirit world, do you, when you and your three pigs tore the golf place all to hell? You think the spirit world'll be impressed by that?" She actually buried her face in her hands and let loose a gut-bucket kind of growl from her chest. "Which ear is it these ideas sneak into your head through? 'Cause you need to plug that one. You need to plant taters in that ear and block it shut for good."

Well, there's only so much of this blame a person wants to listen to. Nobody cares for getting belittled by a person you've had sex with. A person you've licked all over. Nobody wants to sit there and get run down *too far* by somebody who gives them a hard-on. Just about nobody does, anyhow.

A batch of kids attempted to get Biscuit to catch their Frisbees for them, but he didn't give a damn for that, just let them fall and followed his nose toward burgers. He got to circling around a metal grill several tables over, but I could see him. He scooted between legs and so on, got petted a few times, wagged his thanks. Then he got just to the side of the grill and stopped and his back got all humped up. His back humped and it looked like even his hairs became tense from straining and he developed, I swear, a true grimace. He made quite a face. The mutt humped and strained, then pinched a loaf. He pinched a loaf right there almost underfoot. Relief showed quick in his face. He had another loaf ready to pinch when he was seen and empty cans started bouncing from him, and loud

unhappy words were shouted. Biscuit fled, mighty confused, I suspect.

I suppose the three of us all had been watching.

Jamalee stood and clapped for the dog.

"About time to choo-choo," she said. "Why don't we
go on and do something about it?"

20

Pretty International

We tracked the first important figure we knew of to his office, his tow-truck office, over past the stockyards but short of the train tracks. The office was in a vintage garage from the days when cars were narrow so garages were narrow to where they look like playthings to us from now. Tall, narrow doors and a low ceiling and a great big picture window. The old ones made the place with riverbed stone and made it to last. The man had his name above the door, branded in thick loopy cursive on a planed and varnished hunk of driftwood, I believe, that had been hung up there. *Abbott Dell. Towing and Repair.*

When I parked, Bev jerked the car mirror around and

aimed it at her face, then pushed her lips just about smack against their reflection. She worked her lips out hard in the mirror, stretching them wide, stretching them tall, puckering them tight, then got her lipstick out and started drawing. The color she applied I couldn't name, though it was in the pink tradition, I'd say, but above the average pink in pizzazz, like a pink that had been drinking gin since lunch and wanted to dance. This color put some fizz on her face and seemed to make her hair and eyes look trampy and bold.

Jamalee said, "Ask him the questions sort of from the side at first, not head-on. See if he'll let something slip."

"Uh-huh. I could do that, hon. I certainly *could* do that. Or I could be an *a*-dult and flat ask the questions I'd *appreciate* answers to."

"Aw, suit your fuckin' self."

"You look mighty fine," I said, which I meant.

"Thank you, hon. When they get to panting for you, why it's not so hard to steer them some."

Bev got out of the Pinto and went toward the office. She slipped some comely wiggle-waddle-wiggle into her walk. Her dress was a size low or so and she got that white fabric slamming from side to side like it was a sack she'd trapped a poodle in.

She knocked on the glass of his side door and he bellowed a happy bellow when he pulled it open and got a look at her. It was the middle of the afternoon but quiet because, I imagine, of the holiday it apparently was. She spoke and Dell leaned to her, then slid his eyeglasses off and put them in his shirt pocket.

The man didn't look like much. Do coroners pull down big side money? He didn't look like he did. He looked about like one of those fellas who when you're broke and on foot in Dallas or Natchez or Jackson you don't even think about how maybe you could rob them. You let them walk right on by through the dark parking lot. You don't even bother to check if anyone is watching or rehearse whatever stupid bone-chilling line you might use. No, he just looked like a fella who drove a tow truck but had lots of friends who voted.

You see, I know, that since Jason had died with help it fell to scum such as us to prove it. The good world hadn't taken much notice. The ripples hadn't reached them. There was not much official interest in the so-what death of a fella like Jason from an address like Venus Holler. If any rocks were to be kicked over or harsh questions asked, it'd fall to such as us to do the kicking and the asking, which it wasn't much like our prior personalities to do.

The door shut when they went in.

I admit I was tickled at the idea of such as us doing the correct square thing, seeking justice, don't you know, setting a wrong right. It hinted at more direction and purpose in life, I suppose, than I'd ever been saddled with before. I had this daffy notion I maybe *could* imitate such a person.

Me and Jamalee went over the street to the shade and sat on a step below an empty store over there.

Blinds lowered down the door glass and were twisted shut.

She'd forgot her cigarettes and I had one in the shade over there, watching for them through Dell's big picture window.

Jamalee laughed when the blinds also fell across the big picture window. She laughed and poked me with her fingers a few times.

"Don't sulk," she said.

I lit a fresh smoke from the butt of the first. I flicked the butt at a light pole and hit it with a spray of sparks.

"Don't act surprised," she said. "Bev has always been sort of a kind of a kept woman, Sammy, only nobody keeps her more than overnight."

I imagine all of us who are like me grow up with our own ticking bombs planted inside us. You know, the bombs of anger, fear, resentment, and plain ol' not liking yourself to a healthy depth. Some of us carry the complete bunch. Sometimes the ticking from that bunch of bombs is so loud you can't hear another word.

I said, "I guess he figures he's hot shit, don't he?"

❦

When Bev came out of that side door her hands were busy bringing herself back to order. She gave tugs at different aspects of her attire, you know, the hem, the bust, the sleeves. Places of that type. Those blinds had been down most of an hour. Over half an hour, anyhow. Her hair had mashed-down spots in it the way forest weeds and stuff get mashed where deer sleep. The pink had passed away from her lips.

The door shut behind her without me seeing Dell, which maybe was good for him.

There were these celebration balloons overhead, the kind with people in them, riding inside wicker things sort of like clothes hampers, somewhat, or laundry baskets. They sounded the way I expect dragons would. These short flames burst out with a dragon-hiss sound, but around the sides of the hiss you could hear people. They mainly suggested folks on the ground wave up at them or went *Yahoo! Yahoo!* There were five balloons up there in happy colors but they didn't maintain a formation or design of any kind. I can't say yet what that holiday was about or how the balloons fit with it. They flew right along Broadway but well above it and added to the sky like dime-store jewelry on a clean young neck.

Bev gave a look up but kept her feet shuffling, moving slow-footed toward my sunburned Pinto.

"Been busy," I said, "ain't she?"

Jamalee patted my shoulder, a crooked slight grin on her face. She came across close to tender toward me all day that day.

"That's the way Bev lives, Sammy. You've got to get to where you're pretty international in attitude toward what she does. Pretty international toward the ways of the world, and all that."

I flicked another butt and appreciated the hostile burst of sparks.

"Something about her nails me."

"I suspected that," she said. She chewed her lips for just a nibble. "I've got everything she's got, you know, only without all the mileage."

"You say."

We crossed the street from the shady side to where the car waited in the heat. I caught a whiff of myself with the breeze in my face that said I needed a prompt visit to a shower stall. Bev slouched by the car with her hands on her hips.

"Where are my goddam cigarettes?"

"I got 'em."

"Give, Sammy. Give *fast*."

I did and she got one burning.

"Well?" went Jamalee.

"Well, nothin', hon."

"What do you mean, nothin'?"

"I mean Mr. Dell didn't spill any beans to speak of."

Her voice stayed in the dull tones, flat.

I said, "You mean you sexed him down and everything and the big shot *still* didn't show you the file?"

"I wouldn't say I sexed him down, hon."

"I mean, you fucked the dude."

"I didn't *fuck* him."

"Aw," I said, when I understood. "Geez, Bev."

"Look—practically *all* men respond to french."

Jamalee stood there giggling giggles with space between the giggles where I guess she was trying not to giggle.

"But *he* didn't?" I said.

"Oh, he responded, okay, but he didn't *say* anything."

You know, the thought I had right then was of that glass case she had crammed full of cocktail glasses. Her souvenirs of sheet-twistin' and titty-pinchin' with fellas whose names were quickly lost but still those ol' cocktail glasses were there in her front room to hint at hot trips she'd had sex on in the past and also be drunk from on occasion. Each name and each glass alone made me twitch sort of jealous, but all those glasses all together the way she had them meant I had to face it as the mere truth— Bev's datebook had not ever been filled up with prayer meetings. It was the way her life had long been and remained.

Yet I twitched slightly still.

"You didn't see the fuckin' file?"

"It's not here. It's in the coroner's actual office."

"You didn't see the file, and that slug got a blow job?"

"Oh, you *know* I'm a whore, hon. You've understood that all along—ain't you?"

The noise of Jamalee's giggles ran together then, like the noise of those ticks in my head.

"A *free* blow job," she said; then the giggles made her gasp for air. "Which is, which is by *far* the *worst* kind—huh, Bev?"

Bev finished her smoke and dropped it and mashed it.

"Laughter," she said. "Such a wonderful sound. If I wasn't a whore, why I'd've gone into the laughter *business*, vaudeville or whatever. *Hee-Haw.* The *Tonight Show.*"

"Is the big shot still inside there?"

She came near and laid an arm around my shoulder.

"Sammy, I know you want to go beat it out of him or something. You want to beat on him till he tells all. I *know* that's how you're thinking. But that won't do, hon. It *won't do.*"

"It's done before."

"Why don't you drive straight to jail instead and book yourself in for a good long visit. 'Cause you touch that man, Sammy, and you'll be on the spot *real* soon."

Jamalee had quit giggling. She also came near and rested a tiny hand on my arm, just up from the wrist, so I could feel her tiny fingers squeezing.

"Aw," I said. "Where's this office at?"

You know the way in which so many official places favor doors with glass that appears steamed over for good by a long shower and usually have a name in block letters on them? This one was that way. The door faced onto a cement walkway that came off the square and ran from the corner like a canyon, sort of, only with various shops and shit on both sides. It was a narrow place, and when I deposited my fist through the steamed glass the glass sprang loose in shards and fell back inside the office, but you could hear the tinkle carry awful clear down the canyon. The holiday situation suggested nobody was around to hear, but that was only a suggestion. Three punches were required. My fist had been wrapped in my shirt, which was checked by black and white checks, but still blood got drawn from my knuckles and rose up slow through the white checks like a bad red dew.

The women both stood several paces behind me, as if to say could be they know me and could be they don't, and while I watched the red dew rise from my knuckles, Bev said, "That's how you do it?"

"Yeah."

"You do burglary like that?"

"You just saw me. I'm kind of directly to the point, I reckon."

"It's a wonder you don't get caught."

"Oh, I *get* caught."

"I don't doubt that you do, hon."

"I've *been* caught, I mean, now and then."

"I've become convinced of that, hon, watching you."

"It happens," I said. "Like winter does."

Jamalee said, "*Hush.* This is not the time for this conversation." Her head was in a steady spin, eyes frittering the landscape up and down and around us. "Let's get in and get out, huh?"

It was dark in the office. I leaned my head in through the broke window and scanned the dark. A car I could hear was going around the square with a loud radio. I bounced up and down a few times to get limber, then bounced hard and hurled myself up and in through the window. The gals both sucked their breath in and held it. I bounced myself in at an angle, I guess, and came down to bounce again from a swivel chair, first, then into a giant brassy spit-bucket sort of thing that had umbrellas grouped together in it. That thing went tumbling in the gray light there and resulted in some clattering as the umbrellas broke loose and slid away, plus maybe a groan from me.

Jam said, "You should've landed on your feet— shouldn't you?"

"Naw. That's what I've got this head for."

Truly, it was not all that dark in there. Light washed in around the closed blinds and in a few seconds it didn't seem so dark, just murky. It didn't amount to an office you'd dream of being given. The desks were that crappy metal type that cheap-ass government outfits get stuck with. There were two of them, and two flags crossed together high up on one wall. A bunch of leaders, I imagine, had their pictures hung; I know one was a Kennedy, the main Kennedy, the shot-in-the-head Kennedy who has got famous as a poon hound, also. Bev's asshole friend had himself in a few photos there, holding up decent-sized fish and so forth, standing in bunches with the rednecks who voted him in.

I went back to the busted window.

"Now what? Where do I look?"

"Try," Jamalee said, with that tone that says you ain't too swift, is you?, "the file cabinets. They're probably gray or black."

"I see them."

"Good. That's good."

"But try them how?"

"Come on. By the alphabet."

"A B C D—which?"

"M for Merridew. Jason Merridew."

I never had experienced an office job or anything of that nature, and I had some questions. "They could file them according to something else, like where they were found. Or what they died of: D for Drowned."

"No," she said. "They couldn't."

She was on the money. I found it in under a minute. The file on Jason was right there handy in the M section of an unlocked cabinet. The folder felt thin; not too many pages seemed involved. I looked inside and saw a sealed yellow envelope and some papers that were typed on all over.

Bev and Jam had their heads stuck in where the steamed glass had been, watching me.

"Help me out."

They both yanked an arm of mine and got momentum for me then lost control and I went flop onto the concrete and maybe groaned again. I stood and tried to look them in the eyes, give them a nasty look, but neither let me. They ran their eyes elsewhere.

We started down the canyon away from the square. I'd left the Pinto down near the Tiny Spot Tavern to blend in among other junk heaps.

"Give me that folder," Bev said. "It says OFFICIAL right on it. We can't walk through town carrying that."

"Probably not," I said, and gave it to her.

She raised the front of her white dress to chest level, showing off her emerald panties, then flattened the file folder on her son's murder flat against her tummy and planted a few inches of it inside her panties, then dropped that dress back down.

"Now," she said, "we can go."

I carried my shirt as we walked to catch the blood from my knuckles. At the car I tossed the shirt into the backseat and gave those knuckles a lick.

"We'll need supper," Jamalee said. "I'm about to fall over, I'm so hungry."

"*Mmm-hmm.* I'll tell you what," Bev said. "You-all go clean up and cool off, and me too; then I'll get a bucket of chicken from Tim, and we'll eat out under the shade tree while the sun sets."

"I'm there," I said. "What about this file?"

"Oh, we'll read it on full stomachs, hon. In case we need to puke, there'll be something down there to come up."

"Oh, God," Jamalee said. "*Good* thinking."

21

Haunt and Run Me Ragged

I stepped squeaky clean away from the shower, wearing a white towel as a skirt, and she was there perched on the edge of Jason's bunk in a purple robe looking deep.

She said, "Did you ever realize the future could be cut in half at any time?"

The shades were pulled shut to mute the sunlight. The color of light in there fairly well matched beer in a glass that set out since yesterday and lost all its bubbles.

"That would still leave half," I said. "I never dared hope for that much."

"It's such a kind of shock. The future always had me and him in it *together*." Jamalee's hands were kneading the blanket, pushing and pulling. "Every picture I ever had in my head that was forward from here had *him* in it with me."

"What happened was awful," I said. "Might be we'll find out who was behind it."

"Sammy, you know, you're taking lots of chances for us over this. You've jumped straight in. You're running some risks."

"Aw, well, shit. Jason was one of the bunch that would have me. You've got to hang tough for folks from your bunch."

"Not so many would the way you are."

"Also, there's nowhere else for me to go, not really."

Jamalee fell back on the bunk and stared up at the underbelly of the bunk where I slept. That purple robe cleaved open some and flashed a good spread of leg flesh. Then she rolled over and rolled the robe around herself and made eyes at the near wall. The smell she released reached over to me and whispered and made a good impression.

"All the tomorrows were planned around *him*. He was the beautiful one, the one with special talent, the one who could just stand in the right spot somewhere else and have the *big breaks* in life flock right to him, practically rip him to shreds trying to be crucial to him."

Around then I sat on Jason's bunk. I faced the other

way from her, showed her my back if she looked, which I'd say she didn't.

"His specialness might be what got him hurt," I said. "Because he *was* fairly well special, at least for these parts."

"For any parts."

"Probably."

I went over to the windowsill where I stored a few smokes I'd pinched from Bev. I held the shades parted a slit wide. There was a two-year-old outside in the road in one of those little cars you pedal and the wheels squeaked and rattled as he went past driving crazy. I fired up and leaned toward the screen so as to blow the smoke outside.

"Sammy, wouldn't you like to add up to something? In the future? Amount to *something*?"

The smoke only partially went out the screen; most of it hitched a ride on the breeze to come directly back at me.

"Naw. I just figure to roll on, stackin' days, you know, till the day I fuck up big enough the future gets canceled. Or else all planned out for me, maybe. There's a somewhat likely chance of that."

"Man, Sammy, I can't live thinking that way."

"Well, I don't *think* about it."

"Uh-huh. It seems you've got you a talent for not *thinking* about stuff."

"It's just clear sight, Jam. I see what I see and don't

need to think much about it. I wouldn't claim it's a *talent*, but I always have had it."

I went away from the window then, toward the john. I stood near the crapper, tapping ashes into the bowl of water. I reckon I'm no better than folks say. Could be I'd like to be, or not, fuck, who knows? After my last puff I let the butt fall like a MIG airplane I'd shot down in the high skies over Bull Shoals Lake or somewhere. I watched for survivors in the lake, but none made it, and I went on back to the room.

She laid there curled on that bottom bunk like a lonely lonely spoon so I spooned myself over her spoon. I spooned so my pecker nudged her ass. Her li'l ol' lovely ass. We made spoons as the flat yellow light shaded into dusk. She didn't scoot away. She didn't scoot but she tightened herself tight in response. Her body felt like furniture or something.

"Is it time for this?" she asked.

"Seems like."

"Everything's not about sex."

"A good bit is."

A sound of claws scraping shingles fell from the roof. The claws sounded like an upset tiny hailstorm zinging across the shingles, then circling back in a frenzy. Probably this noise was of a cat trying to kick a fox squirrel's butt up there. The tiny hailstorm leaped from

the roof to the shade tree and made the limbs click
together.

Jamalee twisted her shoulders about, her body bump-
ing me back, trying to clear her some elbow room. I pulled
away from her a tad and she twisted over onto her
back. The purple robe bunched around her waist like a life
preserver.

"Hot," she said. "Awful hot."

Her tomato head came up as she sat up and she undid
the robe, yanked it loose, and pitched it to the floor. Her
tomato flopped to the pillow again and, God, the entire
dictionary of feelings came into play inside me in various
parts. I'm a person who digs good smells and she had herself one. Her eyes were open about halfway. She laid there
an itty-bitty beautiful small person with thick untended
pubic hair that was brown.

I let my bath-towel skirt fall.

She spun into a spoon again and I followed her. Bones
in her ribs and shoulders came through her flesh clear and
easy to trace. To me she was special and all, but she didn't
carry a chest rack like her mom did, or have that real lush
type of behind, but still she was special and all, I think, in
a different lean bony way.

I slid my hand past the crack in her ass, from the rear,
there, and got a hold on her snatch with a couple of fingers and rubbed. I added in several neck kisses and groans

of gratitude and wonder. My fingers rubbed as on a lucky coin or something, a rabbit's foot or silver bullet.

"Be good to me," she said. "Or bad."

I worked a finger in her. It wasn't like dipping into a spring or anything. She wasn't juiced up with desire exactly. I pulled my hand back and spit on my finger and sent it in again, which went better, slightly. She had a few sounds in her throat that I guess were meant to encourage me but didn't.

"Look," I said, "we don't *have* to do this."

"Hey, Sammy, listen—I'm a human, too, myself. I don't want to be alone, you know?"

Her comment just then planted the happy hopeful notions in my head that would later come to haunt and run me ragged. They were planted with plenty of bullshit to grow on and certainly did.

"That thought has appeared in my mind also."

"So, Tarzan, what gives?"

Well, it got to be skin on skin and she put a rubber on me with an awkward grip and I climbed on and the thing got going. She made some grunts I couldn't decipher. She laid still as though I might miss the target if she wiggled or thrashed or even pumped along at a slow pace. Her eyes were rolling up like an accident victim. The kind you see laying alongside the highway on a stretcher, eyes wobbling, dealing with their fresh concussions.

"Oh, baby," she said.

"What?"

"Oh, baby, baby."

When it happened, nothin' much happened. The bare minimum of joy got harvested. Uh, uh, uh, then I squirted; she made a noise and hopped away and went to the john. Pretty soon I heard dishes rattle in the kitchen.

I helped myself to another of Bev's cool menthol cigarettes. I walked to the kitchen, toward the rattling dishes. Jamalee was inside one of her tents, a green tent. I got close and tried to hug her from the back and she came stiff to attention until I stepped away.

This mood was not the mood you hope for after sweaty business has gone on. It was as if from lifelong spite toward her mother she'd made a pledge to never enjoy sex much. I'd say her mom kind of got the better end of that stick.

Jamalee popped the fridge open. I looked out the screen door and saw it was full dark with fireflies out there; then I saw the candles flickering across the way on a card table in Bev's backyard. I believed I could smell fried chicken.

"Uh-oh," I said.

Bev sat beside the card table of food under the tree behind the flickering candles and spoke: "Did you all get yourselves washed real *good* and *cool?* I surely *do* hope you did. Because it has just been skillet-hot out here *waitin'* on you. You all do *look* like maybe the heat *has* been at you, though. Goodness knows it's been at *me* pretty rough. Don't you know heat this high makes my temples *throb*, then *pound.* Throb and pound. Throb and pound. You *do* look a touch flushed, hon. Both of you do.

"I hope the two of you-all won't have to feel all that *throbbin'* and *poundin'* like me. I'd hate to see that— a mother always hopes her children will have it better than she.

"Now, as to hunger, for *food*, you all just help your-selves to whatever's left of the feast that the flies didn't shit on too much already. I've been waitin' a good long while, throbbin' and poundin', and there's been flies and bugs about aplenty.

"Now, ol' Biscuit has ate extra good in the past hour. Beer, Sammy?"

"Damn straight. Thanks."

The beer rested in a bucket that had earlier been full of ice but now was slightly cool water. The fact that Bev had brung beer, too, shows you so clear where her heart was at. I didn't feel real tall in Bev's eyes at that instant, but I had a rugged thirst on.

For a while me and Jamalee *did* eat. Bev smoked smoke after smoke and tossed back glasses of wine. We all said hallelujah when a breeze shuffled by. Only drumsticks and wings were left. The abandoned cats started circling. The file folder was on the table, I noted, underneath the potato salad dish.

Jamalee didn't say a word for quite a spell, only chewed and swallowed, staring at Bev.

Then came a point when she flung her attitude back at Bev: "Mom, does anal sex hurt?"

"No more than it should, hon."

"Mom, did you used to get more money back in the days when you used to swallow?"

"Oh, goodness gracious, yes, hon. More of *every* good thing—most of which went to you and your brother."

A mouthful of beer right then somehow squirted up my nose and made me spew and hack for breath.

"Mom, did I ever tell you how much I appreciated all the sacrifices you made for your kids?"

"Why, no. No, you never have."

"Good. I'm glad to hear that."

"Oh, I agree, hon. I'd rather you *don't* lie to me."

I said, "Those cats sure are throaty at night."

"Huh. See, so often, *Mom,* I've wished you *would* have lied to me."

"Well, when you get to be an *a*-dult, baby Jam, maybe I'll be able to explain things to you in words you understand."

"I think I understand the words that apply to you, *Mom*."

"You've set quite a spread here, Bev."

"I'll bet my sweet left titty that you *don't*, hon. Not nearly."

"Funny thing, I'd say the potato salad tasted best."

Anyhow, a certain kind of quiet set in there for a short time that was mostly all tension with smoldering edges and loved ones having thoughts they'd like to scream at each other but didn't.

I felt a huge togetherness with him seeing him dead in the pictures. The camera didn't give his body much of a break—it caught the horrid aspects and the homely smallness of it all. The pictures were dealt out the way solitaire is dealt out along the carpet beneath Bev's brightest lamp, and they told a story that made you want to slam your hands over your ears and run with your eyes squeezed shut. Jason laid there dead in each and was seen from several angles. He laid there sogged from pond scum, his hands hovering stiff above ground, the fingers spread, two fishhooks shining snagged in the web between thumb and forefinger. His hands seemed in death to be attempting a little gesture, barely started toward a wave, maybe, or that palms-up move that means stop! Stop! Stop!

"No," Jamalee said. "Huh-uh. I can't see more of that. I can't."

There were sniffles and such from Bev's green chair.

"Broken arm," she said. "Broken *arm*. He didn't break his arm in that pond the way they say."

The dog stood at the door, whining to come in.

"If he died over golf . . ."

Wires from different worlds were crossing in my head and I got static as a result. Incomplete murky ideas garbled to me.

"Well," Jamalee said, "there's also the fellas you snitched on in days gone by."

"Don't say that. Shut up about that."

"Plus," I said, "your run-of-the-mill queer stompers. This town has them like any other."

"But if he died over golf . . ."

I heard myself say, "Anybody at that club knows about any rough stuff it's goin' to be that tush hog that sneak-punched me. That puts me in the right mind to do the thing that needs doin'. I believe I'm goin' to drop in kind of sudden on that motherfucker. I'm goin' to ask him *direct* questions. If the answers test out wrong I'll shoot that motherfucker. I'll hurt him so bad to where his *grandchildren* fall over in heaps. I'll make God hisself ask me to go a li'l easy, please. And I'll disregard God's please, too, most likely."

The only sound for a minute came from Biscuit, still whining. The photos on the floor shined, reflecting the lamplight like a spread of mirrors you didn't want to look in.

Then Jamalee says, "Oh, hell, yes. I'd say that's a plan. Plan enough, Tarzan."

22

Skull and Rags

You know it, too, how so many times when you enact something that turns *extra* big-deal wrong it wasn't what you set out to do at all, or even had in your mind or the back of it. Sometimes you just paused to say, Hey, man, how you been doin'? or maybe you'd say, Just pay me when you get it, or, Do you love him? There was no misdeed in the forefront of your intentions, just skanky chance and nasty chemistry and the wrong words conspiring at you, then *click-click, bang-bang*, and what you have done wasn't what you'd had in mind to do that day but it sure enough got up in your face and happened.

Oh, what a shame.

Mercy, mercy.

At those times you puke and guess God is merely a meddling sort of pissant warden with a series of teachy and insulting events planned that will make or break you, bring you in meek to be loved like a dumb soft lamb, or throw you away for good to continue life unloved on the planet as a loner mutt who'd rather bite a lamb in the ass than lay beside one.

That coin when it comes to you only has the one side and you wake up every dang day livin' on it.

That morning I woke smack-dab there again.

Jamalee had a mood on that influenced me from the kitchen. Her stomped footsteps were complaints meant to stir me from bed. The dishes rattled like questions she wanted to ask of me in a sort of brittle tone, I think.

I figured nerves had rubbed raw in her overnight, as this was the day we'd said we'd wave Rod's pistol at a select citizen or two and provoke some breathy answers. I got dressed, then reached high in the closet, past the stacks of old shoeboxes and such, and pulled down the pistol. I checked the clip and the chamber, then tucked it into my belt line and wore it with the butt sticking up.

Straightaway I could feel that I walked different.

The sun slammed bright light and tough morning heat into the kitchen. The heat helped release odors. Jamalee wore black pants pegged at the ankles and clingy in general, with shower sandals and a red T-shirt that left her belly out to be seen. She leaned against the fridge and was drinking a glass of root beer without ice.

"No coffee again?" I said.

"No. There's root beer, it's got caffeine."

"I can't take it warm like that."

"*Tsk, tsk. Somebody* didn't refill the ice tray."

The first smoke of the day was lit.

"It might not've been *me* that didn't."

"Huh-uh. That doesn't work, Sammy. If it wasn't *me*, which it wasn't, it *had* to be *you*, which it was."

"Yeah," I said. "I see the math there. Okay, want to whip me for it? Want me to bare my butt so you can whack on it?"

"No, huh-uh. That's actually a part of you I've decided I don't care to ever witness anymore. We'll forget that one hour of that one day ever happened. Please? That's what I'd prefer, at least."

"Geez. Was it, was it, what? Awful? Scary?"

"Let's not review yesterday's lesson, Sammy."

"I said we didn't *have* to, you know. I *said* that."

A train was coming too close to be talked over, and we stood there each stuck in our pose, staring, while the tracks screamed and the shiny wheels kept crushing onward. The shack vibrated and hummed like a cheap gadget that had just been plugged in and was already defective.

She said, "I never even truly thought about doing things by myself before. Before Jason got killed. Before then I never had, but I sort of have now."

"You ain't alone, Jam."

"I'm not?"

"I'm right here."

"Aw—you're with Bev. Because of the sex business."

"We can do without that. We can be together the way a certain style of brother and sister are. Or old folks. *We* don't *need* the sex."

"But you *men*, you've *got* to have your sex stuff. *Got* to have it."

"So? Your mom, Jam, she really knows how to do, believe you me."

"I don't care to feature that picture in my head, Sammy darling. I don't care for that *at all*."

I ran tap water over the cigarette stub, then dropped it into a bean can that stood on the stove. There came a cat yell right then, and a second later Biscuit hustled to the screen door, wanting in fairly bad. I bounced the door open with a boot toe and held it for the sad-sack mutt.

"But," I said, "we're still *tight*, right? You and me?"

"Well, yeah. I suppose. We're still *something*."

"We're still tight, that's what."

"We're around each other a bunch."

I went ahead and had a cup of warm root beer. The bubbles helped me drink it down. I fired a fresh smoke and looked at the cup and dreamed it into a cup of rich black coffee. The smoke helped the dream almost work.

The phone rang on the wall there in the kitchen.

Jamalee answered, and her eyes rolled and her shoulders fell.

"Uh-huh, yes, this is Mrs. Pelkey. . . . Uh-huh. They're doin' fine, just fine. . . . I didn't fill it out? Huh. Could you mail it? With all these kids in summer and no car it'd make a hardship for me." Jamalee stood by her crib sheet of details taped to the wall, her eyes scanning up and down the list of facts. "That's Nova. . . . Yeah, she's just great. . . . That's cleared up. . . . Lita and Troy, right."

A burst of voices came from the side yard, the tone of the voices asking for attention, and our eyes met in the kitchen.

I whispered, "Hear that? Is that Bev?"

She said, her eyes narrow, "But—but really it'd make a *hardship* for me. Three kids and no car on foot in this heat." She used her hand to wave me toward the door to look out. "Well, I'd be sure and mail it straight back to you."

It was Bev in the yard in only her red naughty-nightie with William the John Law marching her this way. He had a hand clamped on the back of her neck and he was squeezing. Her face showed discomfort. The sun came clear through her garment and you could see her rack wiggle and a tuft of private hair. John Law was saying things with his mouth real near her ear.

I spun toward the fridge and set that nagging pistol on the top shelf, where the milk would've been if we had any.

Jam said, "Somebody said that? Well, that *somebody* who said that is a liar. A *damn* liar."

The screen door whipped wide and William shoved Bev in before him. The pistol at his hip had his other hand on its butt and the little doohickey was unsnapped.

He gave her a shove and unclamped from her neck.

Bev bumped the stove and kept her eyes down. She seemed to look at her feet, which were grass-stained faintly.

"William has some shit he wants to say."

"*Has* to say," he added. He caught Jamalee's eye, then raised his front finger to his throat and did a slitting motion. "Hang up and listen, kid—*now*."

"Ma'am?" Jamalee said. "Ma'am? My lord—Troy just fell from the apple tree and he's bawling like he's serious hurt. I'll call you, hear?" She put the phone up, then said, "What'd we do?"

"Button up your lip, kid. Don't *even* bullshit me. All of you sit your asses around that table, and keep your fuckin' hands on the top of it, and button those lips. You're fixin' to hear the most weighty words you ever have heard. I'm fixin' to tell you white-trash morons a thing or two that's *vital*—do you know that word? *Vital* to any tomorrows you peckerwoods hope to lay around in and piss and moan the way you trash do."

Bev said, "You're from just barely over . . ."

And he swatted her on top of the head and made a thump.

"Hush!"

I started to rise to take my swing but he eased that pistol halfway from the holster.

"Boy," he said, "if I want I can make you go away this minute. There's hardly a wrong thing that's happened around here you couldn't be found guilty of. You're a natural fit for any flimsy frame, plus there's the stupid junk you definitely *did* do."

He had us placed where he wanted us. We bowed our heads in the heat, hands on the table, ears way open. He had the floor all to hisself and seemed to dig the way his words bounced from the walls and made us cringe.

"You poor silly sacks of shit. You ignorant white-trash scum. One, the kid *drowned*—do you understand? The sissy boy wanted to show off that he was a gay blade and dove in that pond fully dressed and got unlucky. Two, okay, maybe he was tossed in that pond by somebody hereabouts who traced his *disease* back to the kid. A li'l problem in the blood that's been blamed on your boy. Or, could be he asked the wrong ol' hillbilly to let him suck his dick—that's a scene that can go mighty sour, you know.

"Then you idiots go bustin' into offices where you've practically advertised you were goin'. This is causing agitation amongst folks you'd really, *really* rather not agitate. You really don't want to do that.

"Hey! Did I say yet that there's at least three hundred miles of roadside ditches in this county, and that you-all'd be easy to drop in a deep one anywhere along there in all those miles? Did I point that out yet?

"But, you know, hell, Bev, you know I don't *hate* you. You've helped me in the past, been a *big* help, which I appreciate, and I truly would be sorry if them vicious Timlinsons dumped you and yours in a ditch and I had to find you.

"Lord Almighty, I'd rather that don't happen. I'd get awful nervous about my soul and shit, I truly would. But I wouldn't keep it from occurring. I couldn't, not really. Things are in motion bigger than all of us.

"Bev, you know I don't hate you, but I've got to say, sugar lamb, that you-all ain't ever goin' to get bowlegged from totin' your brains, are you?"

Parts of his uniform caught sunlight and brightened.

He had got my head straining to sift through possible decisions I might attempt to follow.

He went to the screen and actually *turned his back* to us, so casual and calm. This John Law was that breed of triple-mean sucker who is so obviously triple-mean he don't bother to act more than irritable.

"Why do you folks do it? Why do you make me come to this point? I'll wager you don't know why your own selves. Nope.

"Or maybe, let's try this one, say this car of some sort whooshes up beside your boy and somebody says to him in this excited voice, 'Hey, pal, your sister's been hurt—hop in and we'll carry you to the hospital.' Say the fella or fellas in that car have serious good reason to have an anger on toward the boy, the boy and his bunch, and there was a lesson to be taught that got out of hand. Say it went that way. Say he was only supposed to get the fear of the Almighty slapped into him. Plus the fear of certain individuals.

"You could never prove nothin'. There's nothin' to prove. An accident resulted, and everybody wishes it didn't, but you and me and the trolls under the bridge know it did." Then he says to me, "Where the fuck are you from, boy?"

"I'm from a different planet, boss. A different planet that happens to also be on this planet."

"I believe I know the spot. I visit there plenty."

You know, the regular well-to-do world should relax about us types. Us lower sorts. You can never mount a true war of us against the rich 'cause the rich can always hire us to kill each other. Which they and us have done plenty, and with brutal dumb glee. Just toss a five-dollar bill in the mud and sip wine and watch our bodies start flyin' about, crashing headfirst into blunt objects, and our teeth sprinkle from our mouths, and the blood gets flowing in such amusing ways. Naw, it's always just us against us—guess who loses?

"Anyhow," he says, standing right by the table with his hands on Jamalee's shoulders, "the main thing is is to stop. Stop what you're doin', or think you're doin'. Stop and button those lips. What nobody wants is a bunch of that word-of-mouth shit runnin' around. A beehive of rumors that only spur trouble. Where's the point?"

I said, "Man, I'm thirsty." I swung my head in the direction of the fridge. "I need a beer. Boss, you want a beer?"

Jamalee said, "Uh, huh-uh, there's no beer left."

"Sure there is. Let me get us a couple."

"I saw you drink the last one."

"Naw, I don't believe you did. I got some more at Lake's."

"I don't want no beer," William the John Law said. "Plus I told you to shut up."

"It's so hot though, boss. How about some root beer? A tall glass of ice-cold root beer?"

"What kind of root beer?"

"Uh, let me go see. I'm not sure. I'll go see."

"Uh-uh. No, no, nope. Just set back down there and let me finish. I'd prefer ice tea from the Howl Cafe, anyhow. It's not so sweet."

"But, boss, this is good cold root beer. I ain't kiddin'."

Jamalee said, "Hush up, Sammy! Sammy, hush up!"

"She's tellin' you right, boy. She sure is. Now, here's the deal, uh, but first I'll tell you: Say you was to go messin' with a bear and that bear gnashes down on your fingers and, hell, you know, that *hurts*, eh? Hurts the bejesus out of you, and plus it's a pity. Now, if you was to go on back and mess with that bear some more and the bear eats you down to where all that's left is a skull and rags—whose fault is *that*?"

John Law gave us the eye, then reached inside his belt and raised a paper sack and held it over the table and poured money from it. Folding money, twenties and fives and their kin. It looked like a lot to me.

"That, folks, is a Valentine's card of cash from folks who'd rather all this hadn't happened. *Sincerely* rather it hadn't happened, which the money proves."

"It's not all big bills," Jamalee said. "There's quite a few fives."

"A hat was passed amongst those who've took pity on you. There's fifty-five hundred dollars there on that table. Let yourselves smell of it."

I said, "And the deal is?"

"The deal is you-all button up your lips forever. You stop stirrin' around in other people's business. You accept this apology. What I'm goin' to do is, I'm goin' to leave this pile of money here with you. Then come tomorrow, see, I'll fall by here and see if you've got enough sense amongst the three of you to see the sensible solution here."

Boss man eased a ways toward the door.

"You want to give that money back to me—then that's on *you*. Understand? That'll make what happens *your* doin'. So you idiots can take the money, or take your chances."

As he went away he sang that song that says there's miles and miles of Texas but sang it with *ditches* where *Texas* belonged. He didn't sing it good, just sang it.

I went fast to the fridge and pulled Rod's pistol, which Bev saw in my hand and her mouth dropped open. I scanned out the screen and watched William slowly get into his car, and slowly start it, and slowly drive away.

I said, "There's ditches his size, too."

23

Your Head in Dollars

The empty house down the road used to once be the grandest sporting palace in the holler, with a porch wrapped around three sides and wide enough to entertain on, dance upon in the night air, cuddle in shadows, and pitch woo at lavender-scented gals who'd willingly play out the corny skit of courtship with a fella but never ruin him finally with the word no. Passing years had knocked holes in that porch, worked it loose from the house so it tilted to earth like a ramp. The house had got sun-washed and windburned to that forlorn gray color that bespeaks history. In a few sheltered corners you could see red paint still clinging, still trying to appear sinful and beckoning to the pent-up horny on long-ago pay nights. There were two full stories to the joint, a peaked tin roof, maybe six or so bedrooms, one huge parlor, and not much kitchen at all. The house was still called Aunt Dot's, and it rode on a hump of dirt but listed leeward like a mighty nice party boat from yesteryear that ran aground and never had gotten raised by any tide and washed back to sea.

"I've got this sick feeling to my roots that we did something terrible," Jamalee said. "Me and Jason and you, Sammy. We acted wrong as a bunch, but he paid the price for us all by his lonesome."

"I'd like to argue with that," I said. "But it'd be a lie."

Our topic to discuss since we left the house had been square citizen stuff—you know, this can't be allowed to pass, this death, the case must make a beeline for the halls of guilt, or whatever they call it, despite all risk or amounts of money, and be made right in the eyes of society who live across the tracks and avoid us. This topic had started over in Bev's front room and run on for a while; then we went strolling for no special reason. Road dust powdered the breeze and the sun was in one of those moods. We walked on past the other shacks, past the stone church that had fallen in on itself when this century was a pup but a few racks of stone are stacked yet at the borders and trace the shape of the dead church like chalk around a body. A couple of crab-apple trees had got inside the old shape and laid down roots and become landlords. Quite a few generations of trash had been dumped down the church storm cellar and stared up.

When we came to Aunt Dot's, I said, "The part of this mess I really, really can't cut is the part where the price is put on our heads. That's a creepy sensation, see, to know there's a price on your head in dollars and it's *kind of awful low*."

"I've taken money for many a thing that was personal," Bev said. She stood there nudging a whiskey bottle left by history with her big toe. They don't make bottles that look that way these days. "But I can't take money for my boy."

"Me neither," Jam said. "The very idea of it is intended to make us want to hang ourselves. Hang ourselves for bein' such scum as would *take* the money."

I said, "Also, take the dough and you've agreed to a price tag on such as us. They could poach the three of us, too, for less'n a new Ford costs. Think about it in those words, huh?"

The pigeons seemed unhappy that we fell by and rattled the walls and shoved off from the house, their feet flecking white grit and pinfeathers from the eaves down our way, then flapped loud overhead, wheeling in swirling irritated circles, showing attitude.

"Aunt Dot's closed before I was even a girl," Bev said, "just a tot. But I knew her. She died, Dot Gowrie, a funny death also." Bev stood there on a patch of hot dirt that shimmered, shading her eyes, her head turning to track the pigeons. Her feet were bare, as so often they were, which I imagine made her feel like a kid on the loose for summer vacation, or somehow provoked forth some sensation of comfort from some soft spot in her memories. She had on a white T-shirt that recommended you eat at that restaurant near the Bootheel where they throw the rolls at you, and blue jean shorts that were frayed. "They said her truck fell off the cement blocks and mashed her while she tried to fix the muffler. A woman in her seventies, could barely walk or see, fixin' her muffler, only she crawled under there with no tools and laid her head exactly under a wheel." As the pigeons landed back on Aunt Dot's caves, Bev closed her eyes and rubbed at them, her face down. "I've put in a call to every-fuckin'-body I ever did know who might have some idea of what to do. What *we* should do. All they all say is to rest. Some say trust in Jesus, some say try and have another baby, and a few said keep your dumb-ass mouth shut and stay out of bigger trouble."

Jamalee said, "We'll just leave that money sit, Bev. We'll let those dollars rest till tomorrow, then fling them back by the fistful at that shit-ass. We'll make him dig *our* point of view, eh, Sammy?"

I didn't say a thing. I was fairly well alarmed and captivated by that wrecked old house. That crippled sagging old *whorehouse*. I looked at the house and it was like looking at a snapshot of a crucial relative you never did know but instantly recognize. Do you know the feeling? The feeling that the picture is looking at you, too, and knows your whole story, even the rest of it, which it might tell you if you kneeled and listened hard.

I misunderstood where I was for a while.

I recalled where later when Jamalee said, "Why not go inside?"

The floors had become incomplete. The good old wood, the slats, or whatever you'd say they were, had been pried out from sections of all the rooms downstairs and rot had gotten at several spots upstairs. You had to surrender yourself to your fate to step around fast in the shadows there. Who knew when you'd fall. There was a bounty of empty beer cans, brands you'd forgotten about, and assorted litter. Pigeon shit had fell down through the upstairs holes and made splatters that built and spread until they were the size of double-cheese pizzas. At some point a shotgun had been exercised inside the place, and big bites of wall and wallpaper had been blown loose and as the shot pattern spread freckles were applied to everything.

Bev said, "There used to be a piano in here. And there were some soft chairs. Several. I took the green one home. Other stuff, too. That's been awhile back, though. Pretty *long* while. The piano even then didn't have any guts left. The strings and stuff had been taken so you couldn't make music anymore but the husk still sat in here. By the stairs, there."

Jamalee stood by a window where the frame had tilted along with the house, the sunlight jumping on her back, and the light lit her hair extra red and her head lowered and raised like a red-sky sun that was trying to stay up late instead of setting. She said, "Would we really end up in a ditch the way he said?"

"Hon, you only hear about such stuff all the time."

"Might as well see what's upstairs," Jamalee suddenly said. "With me?"

Bev said, "Yeah, baby, you're right, we might as well."

Then the two of them led the way around the pigeon pizzas and the trash from the bygones and deeper into the wreck, moving alongside each other, touching sometimes, like best girlfriends who'd begun a fresh strange adventure together neither would've started alone and both hoped not to regret.

I reckon I always had been huntin' for a place to plant my feet and go down swinging.

My craving to be a hero started to swell, and I followed the gals up into the mess with a smile.

24

~

Hang the Blame

The money heckled us and got us itchy so we stuffed the stuff into an oyster cracker box which was then shoved to the far back of Bev's uppermost cupboard shelf. It had seemed unhealthy to our ideals to have those heckling bills of folding money stacked before us on the table, catching our eyes, making mathematics happen in our minds, winking, flirting, courting our weaker sides. Powerful faith in our weaker sides is, I imagine, why ol' John Law left money in such an amount with us anyhow, left it to serve as an agitator toward us accepting his sense of things.

We paced around in Bev's shack and talked and talked but didn't get much said worth repeating.

That cupboard *did* get glanced at quite a few times.

For a spell there was a woman in the road screaming at a house up the way. Her car was running and the headlights were on, but she stood on the road in the light beams with a kid hugging her leg screaming at the dark house in which she felt a husband-stealing slut hid. A slut who could have the sonofabitch, and welcome to him, if he'd make his stinkin' child support payments like a man, though she knew he wasn't much of one, but he could fake it that he was a decent man, couldn't he? For the kid, for little Kenny?

Midnight was close by, and Bev said, "We can't fight them any way but one way."

Jamalee said, "You figure there's even one way?"

Tires howled in the road and I'd missed the response from the house where the slut hid, which I'd sincerely wanted to hear in case her excuse was a good one and I might find a use for it also someday.

"The one way is if we put their secret shit in the street for all to know. We unload all my dirt about folks here to a minister, or a girl reporter, or like that."

Jamalee rocked in the squeaky rocker, making a tune of squeaks that got irritating.

"I know you know some dirt," she said. "You've gathered you some dirt, I'm sure."

I said, "Most times a bullet wins over dirt, don't forget."

"Also, Bev, these days that between-the-sheets dirt doesn't pack the same punch it used to."

"Okay, okay," Bev said. "The hell with it. So we'll cast around tonight and dredge up *something*. We'll show we're not only who we look like we are, not deep down."

At the slut's shack the porch light came on. A dude and a gal came out to the porch and looked up the road, then hugged and laughed. The gal repeated the wife's comments in a tone she'd use with a young child. This provoked snickers and hugs, then the light went off.

A couple of cigarettes after midnight Jamalee stood and yawned, then leaned her head to my chest and hugged me.

"I'll leave you two alone," she said. "I'm beat."

In my dreams I had one I'd had before where it's all rainy and I'm about full grown but on my way to the elementary school in a yellow raincoat and no pants and all these kids with pants and umbrellas point at my legs and hoot and I look down at my bare ankle and for some reason my butt-hole has moved down there and is leaking when I walk so I run and run and come to a raggedy house where the women in it have whiskers and tattoos and won't unlatch the screen door for me.

"You'll track in shit, that's why not."

That dream is a dream I hate. I totally don't care for

that vision in my head, but it has shown there several times and always shocks me awake.

The sun hadn't turned full on yet, but daybreak birds were tuning up their throats with short trills and quick song bursts. Smoke lolled about in layers toward the ceiling. Bev sat in a chair at the foot of the bed, smoking with her knees pulled up to her chest, sort of in a baby ball.

"Sammy. Can we talk? Sammy, you didn't care for what went on with Mr. Dell. You didn't. You felt I'd done you wrong and I want you to know I might do it again at any time."

"I've got to where I'm cool with that."

"*Cool?*"

"I mean I ain't goin' to stab your patrons, or nothin'. I don't *think*."

"That's not exactly cool enough, hon."

"Well, I mean, if *you'll* hang with me I'll hang with *you*."

I fell back in a flop and closed my eyes.

When I came around again the heat had charged in and the sun seemed as bright as midmorning. Bev sat in the chair, still smoking.

"What's the deal?" I asked.

"I've got feelings all stirred up. Things to ponder."

"Uh. Well. Time for coffee, I reckon."

"No, don't get up."

"Huh?"

"Don't get up, hon."

She stood and pulled down her clothes and made a sight I'd never tire of seeing. She posed and so forth and made me stoked with a stiffie, then gave me a jump that must've lasted an hour.

We rolled from bed and shared a cigarette. She followed me to the kitchen. A table chair had been pulled to the cupboard.

"She came in before first light, hon. She wasn't that quiet. I heard her. Don't go crazy, now."

With only my skivvies on I busted out the door and ran to Rod's. It's like I could feel the truth when I stood by her nook. Her stuff had gone away.

The pistol had gone away too.

I split back to Bev's, and thoughts and feelings and horrors banged and clanged and banged in my head.

All my angers revved.

Fears, I guess, did a bit of goading.

"She can't do me like this!" I know I dressed myself at some point about here. "She can't just dump me! She can't just wad me up and drop me in the trash. *No!* I came *all* the way in, you know? I came *all* the way in, there, *here,* and she can't abuse me this way!"

"Sammy, she's got her reasons, I'll give her that."

I knew there was a short crowbar under my front seat.

Something fine had fallen from her eyes.

"There's Rod," Bev said. "I'd say you should leave him be. Looks like he's been drinkin'."

I only looked at her. I only looked at her and she looked away.

I pushed out and went after Rod.

"Hey, buddy," he said. He'd managed a haircut in jail. He looked more fit, too, but he smelled of ten dollars' worth of cheap liquor. "Been celebratin' my good-time early release. What're you wantin'?"

"You seen Jamalee?"

"No. Not for a while."

"How long a while?"

"They turned me loose before breakfast. I wanted to drive over to the Inca Club for a nice *stiff* breakfast, so I dropped the girl down by Towhead's Gas Station. Where the bus stops."

She had said those words that made me have notions, happy hopeful notions; now those notions got to haunting me and running me ragged and furious.

"And, hey, bud, I'll be layin' around here for a few weeks and that means adios to you, my special buddy. Get in and get your shit and get out and have you a good life, hear?"

I hardly did. I hardly did hear. I turned and headed toward Bev's, and Bev stood in the door watching me.

"And, hey, where'd you stash my pistol? Come back here and answer me, peckerwood."

At the door I said, "Give me a smoke."

"I'm out, hon."

"How could you? Huh?"

A long kiss-off sigh flowed from her.

"My baby Jam grew up of a sudden overnight."

Biscuit shuffled to me and sniffed and I believe I had tears ganging up. I touched the mutt, then fled in the Pinto.

I was fixin' to hurt her. Hurt her tiny body.

At Lake's Grocery I flashed that I needed some smokes and turned in. The parking spaces were filled so I kept back and left room for drivers to back out.

I wish she wouldn't have pulled what she did.

A station wagon started up and started to back out, then stopped. The woman hopped out and ran back into the store.

Jamalee was just a lot too holy to herself.

The bunch that would have me, I don't like them to change their minds.

I thought maybe I might catch her bus.

Everybody was buying beer and baloney, picnic stuff. Then finally the wagon backed up, but right at me, so I backed some more. The wagon slowly turned its wheels and pulled away and a fuckin' Toyota that hadn't been there before wheeled in and took my parking space.

Each extra minute that bus went a mile more.

I leaned on the horn and got flipped off by two rough dudes in the Toyota. Beards, caps, dirty shirts, all that funky hard-guy crap.

The crowbar dealt itself into my hand and I sprang from the Pinto yelling. My yells contained threats.

Both dudes got out. The driver grinned a grin you ain't meant to like. He lifted his T-shirt so I could see he had a pistol inside his belt.

"You think I care? You punk-ass canteen turnout motherfucker!"

I wish that road had bent another way.

Seems like there's always some sonofabitch with a pistol. Testing your character, testing your dedication to stayin' alive.

"You think that popgun'll save you?"

"Hey! Hey!"

Tim Lake came quick down the steps.

I wish I hadn't took to smoking.

She probably could about smell Memphis, as that bus spread fumes through the rice and cotton part of Arkansas, the flat region, clattering toward the river.

Tim Lake laughed.

I said, "You cacklin' cheap bastard, put in some parking!"

I could claim that his laugh triggered me. His mouth

jerked open in one of his big long laughs and spit spun a web from top lip to bottom and my arm shot out hard and straight and fast and his forehead met the crowbar flush.

You could look at him when he landed and not need to ask the main question.

The dude with the pistol said, "Oh, man, don't try to leave. Man, you done *mashed* Tim."

A thing I heard a convict say once came to mind and floored me. "A head is just a pumpkin with ears when it smashes."

The ground caught me. I lay back and looked up, and I felt she thought of me then and would remember my name for good, forever. People congregated and gasped. People muttered about me. Some kids edged close to peek down at Tim's mushy head and they paled quick.

The sirens coming to get me let loose with those constant howls, howling my way like official hounds from the next world over.

I worry that the beach is really no place for a girl alone who can't swim a lick.

Hang the blame where blame belongs.

Now you've heard it.